The Long Road Home

SUSAN ROSE JORDAN

D1714742

* * *

Only when we are
no longer afraid do
we begin to live.

-Dorothy Thompson-

* * *

Chapter One

The impact of the massive explosion was deafening, with shards of steel flying everywhere within the cloud of black smoke. The heat was burning her face. She turned to run, but they stood there blocking her path, waiting to deliver the final blow.

She woke to her screams, shrieking at the very top of her lungs. She was lying in a puddle of sweat, the perspiration and tears soaking her eyelashes. Even after all these years, The same nightmare from that day would re-visit her but becoming less frequent.

Katherine's dream of marriage, children, and eternal happiness had been shattered. She wanted the fairy tale, white picket fence and all. They had planned to start a family, but now that would never be. Sometimes, she felt like she was going through the motions in life. She often felt empty, bereft of any comfort, and incomplete.

Muffin, her long-haired gray cat, snuggled up next to her. Her eyes surveyed her bedroom as she lay in bed, gently stroking him. Floor-to-ceiling windows spanned the entire wall, which looked out onto the tree-lined street. The window in the center had an upholstered seat with two long windows on either side. There was a fireplace on the wall opposite her bed where she had placed two Queen Ann chairs with a small round tea table centered between them. She had painted her room in Nantucket tan and accented with fabrics and throw pillows in yellows, blues, greens, and whites. A painting of an ocean scene hung above the fireplace. Her intention in decorating her home was to create a space of tranquility and comfort, for she longed for this, yet the melancholy feeling remained.

It had been burdensome, at first, to learn to sleep alone, but she had figured it out. Sleeping in the middle of the bed was the solution. She liked to think of herself as strong, independent, and self-sufficient, never having to depend on anyone. She was careful not to form close relationships and kept people at bay. Never did she share any personal information with anyone. Her co-workers didn't know her very well, except professionally, and knew nothing of her past. She maintained only close relationships with her grandpa and her cousin Melanie.

Katherine Kelly had moved to Boston several years ago. She had rented a small apartment in Cambridge. Upon earning her Ph.D. from Harvard, she accepted an offer to teach English Literature. She had fled to Boston to escape the painful memories of her past. She could have earned her Ph.D. closer to home but had to leave. Home would always be different. No, she needed to start over in a new place where the haunting memories would not be so vivid. She kept them deep inside until they would choose, without warning, to rise to the top and paralyze her. After all this time, the pain cut just as deep, but its visits were becoming less frequent.

She pulled herself out of bed and walked over to the window. The late spring breeze coming in through the windows felt so refreshing. She loved open windows. Making her way into her bathroom, she washed her face and put on some sweats. She pulled her long, curly, auburn hair into a ponytail, put on her running shoes, and headed downstairs.

"I'll be back soon, little buddy," she called out to Muffin over her shoulder as she headed out the front door for her morning run. She liked to run toward the Inman Square shopping area on Saturdays, just a block away. She would often stop by one of the shops or restaurants after work. She loved to browse and release stress from the day. This morning, she stopped at the coffee shop on the corner to pick up a bagel to have when she got home.

As she left the coffee shop, she heard someone calling her name, running up behind her.

"Katherine, Katherine... wait up."

It was her co-worker, Olivia. She was a staff assistant at the Harvard Library and the person she had the most contact with at school. So that's how they met. She was single, just like Katherine, but flashy and energetic. She had bleached blonde hair worn in a short, high-volume style and wore heavy makeup. Even her bright lipstick matched whatever she was wearing on any given day. She had been born and raised in Mississippi before her parents moved to Cape Cod when she was a teenager. She had an adorable southern accent she had never lost, a heart of gold, and would do anything for anybody. Even though she came from a family of tremendous wealth, there was not a pretentious bone in her body. She was funny and looked for the best in everything and everyone. At 28, she lived life to the fullest and wasn't ever afraid to try something new.

"Hi, Olivia. What's going on?"

"I'm so glad I ran into you, Katherine. I had planned on calling you today."

"Is everything okay, Olivia?"

"Oh, absolutely. I've invited some friends to go to the Cape over the 4th and stay at my parents' house. They are in Europe for a month, so we will have the house all to ourselves. Thought you might like to join us."

Katherine was at a loss for words. She appreciated the offer, but it was out of her comfort zone. She rarely went anywhere and did not encourage relationships with others. However, her assistant, Daniel, constantly asked her to go out on a date. He was good-looking, and she liked and respected him, but a relationship with a man was the last thing on her agenda.

"Oh, c'mon Katherine... you know the saying... all work and no play."

"I know how it goes, Daniel. I'd just as soon be dull. A relationship is just not in my plans right now." But even having said that, he would still go to her office every Friday and find a different way to ask her out.

She had a way out of this. "Oh, Olivia, that sounds wonderful. I'd love to go, but my cousin is coming into town to see me."

"Y'all both come. The house is plenty big. There will be more than enough room for all of us."

"Tell you what, let me check with her, and I'll let you know tomorrow. Will that work?"

"You bet. Talk to you tomorrow. Bye now."

A calm expression came over her face. The feeling of putting her toes in the sand sounded appealing. She hadn't been to the ocean in such a long time. With the significant house, she was sure she could put plenty of space between herself and others. All she had to do now was call Melanie and run the idea by her.

When she got home, she grabbed her cell and called Melanie. She answered on the second ring.

"Hi Kat, to what do I owe the honor of this call so early in the morning?" Melanie said.

"Well, I ran into a co-worker of mine this morning. She has invited us to join her and others to go to her parent's house on the Cape over the 4th of July. We don't have to go, but I wanted to see how you would feel about that."

Melanie gasped, "Oh, my God, Kat, that sounds awesome. Count me in!"

"Okay, let me know once you have your flight to Logan set up, and I'll pick you up," Katherine said

"You got it. Thanks, Kat. Love You."

"Love you more," Katherine said. "Talk to you soon."

She made herself a cup of tea and headed outside with Muffin in tow to her patio and garden. Gardening had always been a passion and therapeutic for her. She curled into her oversized, wicker club chair with Muffin stretched beside her. It was so beautiful this time of the morning. Quiet with only the sound of the birds. Apple trees lined the alley behind the row of brownstones she could see over her six-foot fence. The amount of space was a little small but serene. She had created a brick patio, a sitting area, and planters housed her tiny garden.

Gazing at her flower boxes and admiring how beautiful everything looked as it was blooming made her think of Stewart. The day she met Stewart had been the day her life slowly began to change.

Chapter Two

When Katherine first moved to Boston, she rented a small apartment near the campus. She didn't want to have to drive because she'd heard the traffic was horrific. After she graduated and accepted an offer to teach, she decided it might be a good idea to buy a place to live in and wondered if it might help her feel more connected to the area. This still didn't feel like it was home. It didn't take her too long, with the help of a realtor, to find the perfect place. It was a brownstone that needed much work because of its age but had tremendous character. It was still relatively close to the campus, an added plus. She planned to keep her tiny apartment and live there while her brownstone was renovated.

A co-worker gave her the name of a contractor. His name was Thomas. He was much younger than she had expected, maybe 29, but he had come highly recommended, and she could see why. He had a vision. As soon as she started describing what she wanted, he immediately got it. He even suggested things she had yet to think of. In addition, his rates were very reasonable. Not that she had to worry all that much about money because of the trust fund from her parents, but in addition to that, she was very frugal.

Together, they had re-done the entire interior. It was quite a task, and what a mess it had been. Once it was livable, she had movers bring her things from storage into her apartment.

After finishing the other rooms, Thomas began the demolition of the kitchen.

"If you want, Katherine, I could remove this wall and make your kitchen larger."

"I love that idea, Thomas." He told her what she needed to select and gave her brilliant suggestions on where to go. It involved much running around and was time-consuming but thrilling at the same time. It was as though she was building her first home and starting a new chapter in her life.

Thomas had just finished installing her appliances when she got home from work.

"Wow, Thomas. The kitchen looks amazing. I'm so glad you suggested taking down that wall."

"Hi, Katherine. I'm just finishing up a few small things. But I must tell you, I've never put in a kitchen quite like this before. Everything's very high-end. You must do a lot of cooking."

"I used to, but not so much anymore. When I did cook, I loved it. It was sort of a hobby of mine."

"I bet you were good at it. I'll be able to finish everything up tomorrow."

"Thanks, Thomas. I'll see you tomorrow."

With a warm look, she gazed around the space after Thomas left, thinking of her grandmother. She would have loved to have had a kitchen like this; God rest her soul. She had been a fabulous cook and passed those skills onto Katherine, teaching her everything she knew.

They kept the floors and trim in the rest of the house. They were beautiful, the original dark mahogany wood. She loved how they creaked when you walked across them, just like the ones back home at her grandfather's estate. The downstairs half bath only needed a new toilet, cabinet, sink, and mirror.

Upstairs, a guest bathroom had been added in place of where a large storage closet had been next to the other bedroom. She had painted and decorated and was very pleased with the outcome. Her home was casual and comfortable.

Once Thomas had finished the inside of her brownstone, all she needed to do was finish up a few decorative touches and sew some window treatments.

There was a slight chill in the air, but it was perfect for painting. It was early May, and she wanted to finish her patio area so she could start her garden. First, she sanded the fence boards that needed it. She was painting her fence crisp white. It was not precisely the white picket she had envisioned in her original plan, but it would look nice and clean. She loved that her back door was centered, leading down the steps to the patio. It enabled her to do more with space. Ultimately, she wanted a cozy sitting area, a fire pit, and ample room to plant her flowers.

She was almost finished with one side when she heard someone whistling in the alley behind her house. It was a pretty little tune. "Sweet Adeline" is what it sounded like. A man stuck his head into her gate, which was partially open.

"Well, hello, theya young lady. I thought I'd stop by and introduce myself to my new neighbah. Name's

Stewart Tuckah. I live right next dowah. I was taking out my rubbish and thought I smelled fresh paint." He was a jolly-looking man and looked around seventy. He was no taller than about 5'10", had a round shape, and was losing his white hair. With his fair skin, he looked like he had just come over from Ireland.

"Nice to meet you, Mr. Tucker. My name is Katherine

Kelly. I hope all the noise we've been making has not disturbed you."

"Oh, not at all, Ms. Katherine. It's nice to heah some noise now and again. It looks like you've got quite an enormous project going on theah for a Sunday aftanoon."

"It's a labor of love," Katherine replied. "I want to get my outside space ready for the summer. I love spending time outdoors."

Noticing the pots with flowers all over the patio, he said, "Looks like someone has a green thumb. That's an awful lot of flowas. Wheah do you plan to put them all?"

"I think I'm going to go online and try to find a wooden flower box I can put along the wall with roses. Then, along the curvature of the patio, I'm going to plant azaleas. I think it will balance things out well."

"My wife also loves flowas and has planted pots upon pots since the day we were married."

"Maybe she can give me some pointers. There's always more to learn about planting and the different flower species." She watched as a dark cloud dropped down to shade his face. The same cloud had come down upon her when her life had been shattered. She recognized the expression and sadness on his face very well.

"I'm so sorry, Mr. Tucker. I think I've hit on a sensitive subject by mentioning your wife. Is she still with you? Did she pass away?"

"No apology needed, Ms. Katherine, and no, she did not pass away. She's just not able to be with me any longah. She got early Alzheimer's a couple of yeahs back, so to keep her safe, she needed to go live at a memory facility."

"I didn't mean to pry, Mr. Tucker. I'm truly sorry," she said.

"Now don't worry yowahself about it, and please call me Stewart. Well, I didn't mean to keep you so long. I just wanted to stop ova and introduce myself. Let me know if you need anything. Nice to meet you, Ms. Katherine, and welcome to the neighbahood."

"Thank you, Stewart. It's so nice to meet you, too."

Way to go, Kat, she thought to herself annoyedly. *Your neighbor stops over to welcome you to the neighborhood, and you upset him. He'll probably never want to see my face again.* He seemed like a very kind man. She was sure he must be lonely. How sad for him that his wife had become ill. She could tell by the look on his face that he truly loved her. She suddenly found herself in unfamiliar territory since she had been a recluse for so long. She wanted to help him somehow. There was a time, which seemed so long ago now, that she was the one everyone went to for advice and often comfort, and it made her happy to give it to them.

The conversation stirred up her feelings as well. The demons had risen once again and were cutting off her ability to breathe.

She decided to go for a run. Later, she could quickly finish rolling out the remaining walls.

She pulled her hair up, slipped on her running shoes, and fled out the front door and down the steps to the street. There were no sidewalks and only on-street parking. She took off down Elm Street quickly, determined to outrun the demons.

She eventually slowed down a little and took in the beauty of her street. It was lined with trees of all different kinds. They were very old, and looked like they had been there for years. Her road was so peaceful. It was carved out from the hustle and bustle in other parts of Boston. Just as she got to the end of her street, a car backfired, sending her into a full-blown anxiety attack. The same sound, like a gun going off, that haunted her so often. She picked up her speed, running as fast as she could. The sweat coming from her bones felt like blood leaving her body from the panic and pain.

When she reached JFK Park, she stopped and sat on a bench by the water. She drank some water and concentrated on taking slow, deep breaths. The panic and pain were slowly leaving, just as they always did.

People were out and about enjoying the lovely Sunday afternoon. There were cyclists, people picnicking, playing frisbee, and walking their dogs, or couples pushing their babies in strollers. She felt sad at the sight of the couples with their babies. She needed to leave before she was engulfed by thoughts of the life she had wanted and lost.

As she walked home, she stopped and picked up a salad from Rebecca's Cafe for dinner.

After she ate, she did a little more unpacking. There were still several boxes waiting. While unpacking some boxes in the kitchen, she came across her grandmother's apron. She held it and raised it to her cheek, caressing it. She could not remember the last time she had put the apron on to cook. That was her other life. It was embroidered with pretty flowers and showed its age from years and years of use. When she was a child, her grandmother would fold it in half and tie it around her tiny waist when they would cook together.

It was getting cooler and darker, so she would finish painting after getting home from work tomorrow. She still wanted to search the internet for the type of flower box that would work for creating her oasis out back.

Chapter Three

On her way to work Monday morning, she stopped at the Crema Cafe to organize her thoughts. While enjoying a latte and a bagel, she made mental notes of things she needed to do that day: meet with department heads, organize her office to wrap up everything from the semester, pick up her cleaning, and go to the bank.

She still felt a little unsettled about meeting Stewart yesterday. He was such a nice man, and she felt so sorry for him. She couldn't quite figure out why, but she felt as though she had known him all her life. It must have been so heartbreaking for him to have his wife still but not *really* have his wife. She felt drawn to wanting to help him and somehow comfort him. How she could help him was the question.

On her way to her office, she stopped by Olivia's office. "Olivia, could you do me a favor and pull up everything you can find about Alzheimer's?"

"Sure, Katherine. Is everything okay?"

"Yes. Just helping a friend."

"I'll send it over to you later on."

"Thanks, Olivia. I appreciate it."

It had been a grueling day. Figuring out final grades had felt like closure. It was the last time she would consider each student she'd had in this set of classes. Some of them had done well, and she felt such satisfaction as she watched what they were becoming. They made teaching worth the work. But then there were the other students who failed because it wasn't the time in their lives to learn the content, the ones who didn't have the skills they needed to make it, and some who didn't appear to care. Those were the ones that made it so bothersome for her.

She gathered her things and what Olivia had provided her and headed out the door. Any free time she could muster would be spent reviewing the information Olivia had given her. From what she had heard, certain foods, even certain food items, were known to help people with Alzheimer's.

She took her time walking home and still needed to stop by the cleaners and run some errands. She wanted to get home in plenty of time before dark to finish her project out back, but she still hadn't found a planter for her roses to put on her patio against one wall of the fence. Gran Elizabeth had taught her everything about growing flowers, especially roses. Hers were exquisitely beautiful. She would say, "Now, Katherine, we do not prune these in the fall. Just cut away the deadness gently, like this, and add compost. Stop fertilizing before the first frost and ensure they have plenty of water to protect them from the harshness of winter." Remembering that time with her grandmother put a smile on her face.

Those were some of the happiest days of her life. Having lost her parents to a car accident as a very young child, she had been raised by her grandparents. She didn't even remember her parents. Her childhood had been magical. Her grandparents had adored her, and she adored them as well. A feeling of total warmth engulfed her just thinking about them.

When she entered the door, Muffin came running up to

SUSAN ROSE JORDAN

her, meowing, twisting, and turning up against her legs. He was such a sweet little guy. "Come here, you fluffy little guy." As she scooped him up and hugged him tightly, he rubbed his head against her face, purring loudly. She gave him his dinner and then headed upstairs to change into her old shirt and jeans so she could finish painting.

After changing into her old clothes, she headed back down the stairs and out the back door, stopping dead in her tracks. Surely, she was having a dream. This couldn't be real. She gazed over the entire area and saw that all the painting had been completed. Then she looked at the fencing to her left and was in total amazement. The exact type of flower box she was searching for on the internet was in place, only this one was much nicer. It was custom. Along the back, a piece of a lattice was attached with hooks hung here and there to accommodate her gardening tools. In the very center was a wooden plaque. The words Flowers make the world a better place were carved out: *beautiful* and true words. The flower box was also filled with soil, just waiting for flowers to be planted. If this was a dream, she didn't want to wake up. It was gorgeous. She stood there frozen in time, feeling unworthy of who had done this for her. But who was it? It had to have been Thomas. He knew what she planned for the out-back area and came while she was at work to complete it for her. She called to thank him.

When he picked up, she said, "Oh Thomas, the garden area looks beautiful. I don't have the words to thank you. It's incredible." There was a long pause before he responded. She wondered if he was still even there.

"Katherine, I'm not sure I know what you're talking about. I haven't been to your place since we finished inside."

"Oh, I got home from work today, and a project I started out back was finished. I just assumed it had been you that did it."

"Well, I wish I could take credit for something that has made you so happy, but it wasn't me."

"Okay, thanks, Thomas. Stop by and take a look one day. You'll love it."

After she hung up with Thomas, she stood there in total bewilderment. Then she heard a sound behind her. Stewart was standing at her open gate to the alley.

He stepped inside and stood beside her. "I hope you don't mind, Ms. Katherine. It looked to me like you could use some help."

Tears welled up in her eyes. "Stewart... you did this? I'm speechless. I don't know how to thank you."

"No thanks necessary. Actually, I thoroughly enjoyed myself. It's been a long time since I've done anything like this." He watched with a warm expression as Katherine went over to the planter, admiring it. She was taking it all in and touching every intricate detail. Her hand touched all the words on the plaque. He had made it for his wife. It made him feel happy to pass it on to Katherine.

Without pause, she threw her arms around him, tears rolling down her cheeks. When she let go, she looked up at him, saying, "It's been a long time since anyone has done anything like this for me. It's incredible. I wish I could also do something for you to repay you for your kindness. Please tell me how much you paid for it. I want to reimburse you."

"Just neighbas being neighbas. I'm happy you like it. It didn't cost me a single penny. It's sort of a hobby of mine. I like to make things. Like shelves, stools, small chairs, and anything else I might find interesting."

"Well, you are very talented. I couldn't have found anything this lovely online or anywhere else."

"Thank you kindly, Ms. Katherine. Now, who, might I ask, is this little fur ball rubbing against my legs?"

"Oh, I'm so sorry. Muffin, come here!"

"Not to worry, Ms. Katherine. I love cats—all animals, for that matter. Unlike humans, they ask for nothing but give you everything."

"I could not agree with you more. This is my muffin. He's my baby. He rarely takes to strangers, but he seems to like you."

"The feeling is mutual."

With that, he bent down and scooped Muffin up into his arms. Katherine could hear him purring all the way over to where she was standing. This was such a funny sight to her. Muffin didn't love anyone but her... that is, until now. She couldn't quite explain it, but she suddenly felt like she had just made a very dear friend who would be in her life forever.

"Well, Mr. Muffin, I need to go home now, but I promise to come back to see you again– that is, if yowa mama[1] does not mind?" He lowered him back to the ground.

"We would both love for you to drop by as often as you like. I'm finishing up my semester at school this week. I teach English literature at Harvard. I'll have all sorts of time and am looking forward to it. I'll finally have time to devote to other things I love to do and relax."

"That's wondaful. By the way," he pulled a piece of paper from his pocket. "I want you to have this. It's my cell phone numba. I want you to call me if theya is anything you evah need."

"Thank you so much, Stewart. I'll text you mine as well. Please call me anytime."

"That sounds good, Ms. Katherine. I have to be going now. Enjoy planting yowa flowas."

"Thanks again, Stewart. I surely will. It's going to look beautiful. I can't wait for you to come over and see the finished project!"

After Stewart left, Katherine sat in a chair, pulling her legs up and wrapping her arms around them. She felt warm and fuzzy inside, like she'd just had a soothing cup of hot choco-late. She felt so happy... almost giddy. It was like a part of her old self was trying to emerge. *When was the last time I felt like this?* she mused. As she sat gazing around at the sudden beauty everything was taking on as it came together, her eyes fell upon the apple trees behind her fence. Jumping up, she went inside to grab a basket, taking it and filling it with as many apples as she could reach. Tomorrow, she would put them to good use.

Yes... tomorrow she would cook.

Chapter Four

The following day, Katherine hurdled out of bed. She felt so lighthearted after yesterday and was incredibly enthusiastic about her plans for the day. How odd it was going to feel to cook again.

To finish the semester, she only needed to post final grades, which would only take a few minutes from her home office. She had done most of her end-of-semester work yesterday.

She was so eager to get started that she almost abandoned her morning run but kept to her regular schedule. Running was good for her. It helped her cope. She had never turned to opioids or alcohol to calm herself and never would. If the painful memories from her past crept up without warning, she had and would continue to outrun them.

She had to get to the market. Since she only dined out or ate frozen microwaveable dinners, she had almost nothing in her cabinets or refrigerator. Not even a few staples or spices. She laughed out loud and said to Muffin, "This is going to be a very large grocery order." As he always did, he meowed loudly in response and rubbed and twirled in and out of her legs. Muffin seemed almost human at times. He always seemed to know how she was feeling and would do his best to comfort her. She would certainly need to take her SUV today. It would be impossible for her to carry her shopping bags home as usual.

After showering and making herself look presentable, she headed to the market. It was unimaginable to her that she was actually looking forward to it. The hard shell she had allowed to build up around her for protection, like barnacles attaching themselves to the bottom of a boat, had also covered up her memory of how much she loved to cook.

She arrived at the checkout with a basket almost too heavy to push. The young girl at the register noted it and said, "Just moving in?"

Katherine chuckled, "Something like that."

The back of her SUV was loaded to capacity. She had planned to make apple crisp, a brown-butter apple loaf, and streusel-topped apple muffins. At the last minute, while at the market, she decided to make a shaved Brussels sprouts salad with hazelnuts and apples covered in a brown-butter dressing for dinner. She also picked up a delicate piece of salmon to go with it. She never needed recipes to refer to. Her grandmother had taught her what went well with what and the spices to use to make many things. Exact measurements weren't necessary. "Just eyeball it...," she would say. Remembering that brought a smile to Katherine's face. When she arrived back at her brownstone, she started the unloading process. It was the first time she had regretted having steps leading up to her front door. Even though there were only eight, it still made it quite a chore to haul groceries from the car. Especially since she had not purchased this amount of food in several years. She carried the first four bags up the stairs into her house and set them on the counter in the kitchen. Even though she ran every day, she was not as accustomed to lifting things, especially up a flight of stairs. She started putting away what she had unloaded so far to give herself a rest. While unpacking, she heard Stewart calling out her name from the front door. She walked through the hallway from her kitchen only to find him standing there holding several more of her bags.

"Stewart, what on earth are you doing?"

"I saw you pull up, Ms. Katherine, and it looked like you had a lot of bags to bring in. Thought I might help."

"Stewart, you are one of the kindest men I've ever known in my life!"

"Not such a big thing, Ms. Katherine. I'm shuwah there are lots of nice people out thah that would do the same thing."

Scanning her countertops with his eyes, he couldn't help but notice the massive amount of food. "Are you expecting company or something?"

Smiling back at him, she shrugged. "No, just refilling the kitchen. As you can see, I haven't been to the market in quite some time."

She was unsure why, but she suddenly blurted out, "Would you like to come over for a simple dinner with me tonight? Nothing fancy, just a salad and salmon. Maybe it could be my way of paying you back for what you did for me."

"I would like that, Ms. Katherine. I look forward to sharing yowah company, but please do not feel you need to pay me back. It's something I love doing, and now that I'm retired, it gives me something valuable to do."

"I'm delighted... Does six work for you?"

"Six works just fine, and I thank you for yowah hospitality. Is thaya anything I can bring to contribute?"

"Nope... Just yourself. See you at six, Stewart, and thank you so much for helping me unload my car."

"You are mowah than welcome. It feels good to feel valued and be of use to someone again. I'll see you again at six. Thank you again fowah the invitation."

Thankfully, she had held onto all her dishes and baking pans. She owned many gadgets. The things she had purchased years ago were very well made. She believed that you'd get a better result if you bought quality products. For instance, she only made certain things in her cast-iron skillets. They were so well seasoned and, in her opinion, made things taste better.

She set herself to work, pulling out the ingredients she would need for the things she wanted to bake that day. She wanted to make apple crisp for dessert and buttermilk biscuits for dinner.

She put on her grandmother's apron, and it was as though it had transported her into another place and time. A cool breeze came in through her kitchen window, but inside, she felt incredibly warm. When she began to knead the dough, she closed her eyes and felt a calm sensation come over her. It felt so good to create something again. She had honestly forgotten what a wonderful feeling it was. She couldn't remember the last time she had felt so alive.

It was good that she had put in a double oven; she would need both today. After placing the bread in the oven, she made her apple crisp. This had been her grandmother's recipe, and it was delightful.

She had been puttering in the kitchen for so long; time had gotten away from her. She assembled the salad with shaved Brussels sprouts, crumbled bacon, apple curls, and hazelnuts. The small dining area was through an arched entryway off the kitchen. She set the table and headed upstairs to freshen up.

Stewart arrived at six o'clock on the dot. "Your house smells wondaful. If it tastes half as good as it smells, I'm a very lucky man."

They sat and enjoyed their dinner in her small dining area. She had a round oak pedestal table with seating for four. "Ms. Katherine, this is delightful, and it almost looks too good to eat. And these rolls. Where did you find these? They are the best I evah had."

"Believe it or not, I made them. It's an old family recipe. Thank you."

They chit-chatted as they ate. She had only just met him, but it felt as though she'd known him her entire life. After dinner, she made coffee to go with their apple crisp. She served it in the sitting room. She had put a fake log in the fireplace just before Stewart arrived, and it was burning beautifully. They relaxed in her large, cushioned chairs, sitting across from each other with their dessert, and talked. Muffin curled up in the chair next to Stewart.

She told him about losing her parents and being raised by her grandparents at their estate near Charleston. She told him about her cousin Melanie and how close they were—they had practically been raised together—and all about her horse. They had given her and Melanie a horse of their very own when they turned sixteen. She had named her horse Lucky. She told him about losing her beloved grandma Elizabeth to cancer when she was twenty-four. "How often do you go home for a visit?"

"Not that often, really. My grandpa and Melanie Face-timed me back in January to tell me he had decided to remarry. Her name is Ruth. Melanie stood behind him as he described her to me, doing sign language to reveal her feelings, finger-pointing down her throat, slicing her throat with her hand, and making grotesque faces. She clearly did not approve of Ruth. It caught me between laughing and crying. My grandpa, seeing the look on my face, said, "My sweet Katie, I've had the love of my life in your grandmother. Ruth is merely a companion. I'm getting up in my years and lonely at times. She is a very nice woman and treats me well." I told him I'd support him in whatever he did and that I'd be there for the marriage ceremony."

* * *

It was a simple ceremony in the parlor at the estate with the fireplace behind them. Her grandpa looked very happy, and so did Ruth. She looked nothing like her grandmother. Their grandmother had a soft, elegant look and was very refined. Ruth had an oblong face and green eyes, and her light-colored, tinted grey hair was pulled back away from her face. Although Elizabeth had also been Southern, Ruth was much more country. But, more than even that, she was more of a hillbilly. She lacked the class Elizabeth possessed and did not speak as properly.

Melanie knew her better than Katherine did since she lived close by and saw her often when she was visiting her grandpa. She didn't particularly care for her but could not quite pinpoint why. They both just hoped their grandfather had not made a mistake.

During the simple reception with just a buffet of food, drinks, and a small cake, Katherine noticed a man standing across the room talking to others. He was a tall, nicely built man and had thick, jet-black hair. He had one hand in his pocket and a drink in the other. Their eyes met for a moment, and he nodded upward toward her as if saying hello.

"Mel, who's that man standing over there?"

"That's Russ. He's the caretaker grandpa hired to take care of the horses and virtually everything else that he used to do around here. He came here about the same time as.:." She did not finish her sentence because she spotted someone she knew and went over to say hello to them.

She couldn't quite put her finger on why, but the way he had looked at her made her uncomfortable.

* * *

Katherine suddenly realized that she'd been talking nonstop. "I'm sorry, Stewart, I've been rambling on and on. You've barely had a chance to speak a single word."

"No, no, Ms. Katherine. I've thoroughly enjoyed hearing about yowah life and family. Mine is boring by comparison now that my dear Abby is gone. Well, that's not exactly accurate. She's not gone, just in a different stage of her life. I see her several times a week, and it makes me happy that she's safe and well taken care of."

"That's wonderful, Stewart. You have such a good outlook on life. I admire your strength and the way you've handled her illness. I know it can't be easy when someone you love gets Alzheimer's. It's such a cruel disease."

"When the onset initially happened, I didn't do such a good job. She was so young, it neva occurred to me that she was sick. I just thought she was getting fowahgetful. I'm ashamed to admit that I lost my patience with her more than once. But then things eventually got worse. She stahded doing things totally out of charactah and some seemed somewhat crazy. Like thah was the time in summah that she put her wintah coat on to go foy a walk, and then anothah time during a dreadful storm, she came downstayas wanting to go to the beach." He softly chuckled as he continued, "Oh and I can't foyget the time she went into our next-dowah neighba's house on her way home from a walk and flipped on the television. When owah neighbah walked into the room, Abby thanked her for stopping by and offahed to make her a cup of coffee."

"I guess sometimes it's best to find humor in an unpleasant situation, Stewart. I'm so glad nothing bad ever happened to her. I would imagine having her live in the security of the facility must give you a sense of relief and there's nothing wrong with that."

It had gotten rather late, so they said their goodnights.

"Thank you so much for suppah. I might not eat again for days."

She gave him a daughterly hug and kissed his cheek.

* * *

Over the weeks and months that followed, they got together often. They took walks into town or along the river, stopping at cafes for lunch, and he'd often stop over if he heard her outside. She often went with him to visit Abby. After going over the information Olivia had provided, she discovered the MIND diet. Having learned that blueberries and nuts were good brain foods, she baked blueberry-and-banana-nut whole grain muffins to take to her. Her health seemed to have declined more and more each time she saw her. There was recognition on her face whenever she saw Stewart, although she clearly didn't remember he was her husband. In fact, she had a gentleman friend she referred to as her boyfriend. Stewart was so loving and kind to her and her friend. Stewart had found peace with it, and that made her feel so happy for him and even envy him. Even after years of psychotherapy, she could not put the past behind her. It still haunted her. He didn't appear to have any demons in his life.

As Stewart was driving them home one day, she asked him, "Stewart, how are you able to cope with watching your sweet Abby slowly drift further and further away?"

"It's something beyond my control, and I have no choice but to accept it. Life doesn't always work out as planned, but we have to keep on living. What I want most is to make Abby's last days on the dear Earth as pleasant as possible. If I can do that, then I can be at peace with the rest of it." Katherine nodded while looking at him in amazement before turning her head toward the window, immersed in deep-rooted thought the rest of the way home.

Chapter Five

While sitting out back in her garden and having her morning tea the next day, she couldn't help but reflect on all the conversations she had had with Stewart. She truly admired his strength. She suddenly felt guilty about having a family that she cherished and that was always there for her while Stewart was all alone, losing his beloved wife with no family at all. Life had thrown him a heartbreaking curveball and yet he had dodged it and lived on despite it. He was doing what he needed to do with a tremendous amount of courage.

Curled up, looking at her garden, she was transported back to another time when she was growing up with her cousin Melanie. It was a time when she was mostly very happy.

* * *

Katherine and Melanie were more like sisters than cousins. They were only six months apart in age and had been inseparable growing up. They looked nothing alike, but Grandpa would often humorously refer to them as the twins. While Katherine had curly auburn hair, big brown eyes the color of whiskey, and olive skin, Melanie had blonde hair, vivid blue eyes, and fair skin. She would burn like a beet if she hadn't applied a lot of sunscreen.

Their grandparents, Benjamin and Elizabeth, lived in a large, estate-type home that was said to be historic, just southeast of Charleston, South Carolina. You could see the main house down the lane as you entered the property. It was lined with large oak trees on both sides, draped with moss hanging down from them. On either side, along the way, was the wooden, slatted fencing to contain the horses. The house was white, with tall columns and a deep front porch that ran the width of the house and around the sides. It was on fifty-eight acres of land that eventually led down to the water with a small, soft, sandy beach. The back was just as beautiful and inviting as the front. There were rockers placed on the deep-covered porch to relax on and potted plants everywhere on the grassy knoll for as far as the eye could see. There was a guest cottage a short walk from the main house, down the pebbled path, and not too far from that was the stable for the horses. Their grandmother had planted her rose garden along the side of the house that you could see once you pulled up the lane. They looked like someone had painted them up against the house. They were so very lovely. She had planted other flowers in many locations scattered all over the property. Everything always looked so bright and beautiful. The view could have been used on a postcard.

Katherine was the prissy one, and Melanie was the tomboy. Katherine liked to paint her tiny nails, and Melanie liked to pick up frogs and then torment Katherine with them, chasing her around the ranch. Grandpa would often take them fishing when he went. Katherine would screech at the sight of the live minnows and cry when the hook was put

27

through their mouth. Melanie would grab her minnow out of the bucket in her tiny little hand and hook it herself, with Grandpa's guidance, of course. They would often catch fish to have for dinner that night.

Their childhood at their grandparents' home had been enchanting. Melanie spent more time there with Katherine than she did at her own home with her parents. She had been an only child. Her mother could have been more nurturing but ensured Melanie had everything she needed. Her father was very loving, and they had a special bond. When she was little, she would always race down early in the morning to see him before he went to work. As he had his coffee, he would always let her pretend she was having one, too, but he poured milk into her coffee mug instead. He would always ask for a big hug before he left, sending her back up to her room until her mother was up. At bedtime, he was the one who would read her a story and say her prayers before giving her a kiss goodnight. Her mother was the type that preferred to give Melanie things rather than her time. They liked to travel and thus would often leave Melanie with her grandparents. Her grandmother had decorated bedrooms for both girls, paying no favoritism. The lack of love and attention from her mother had made Melanie independent and resentful. She would always say what was on her mind, giving little thought to it before it came out of her mouth. That would often affect her ability to have close friends, but not with Katherine. They were thick as thieves and had an inseparable bond.

Katherine, on the other hand, had grown up adored by her grandparents. They did everything for her and with her. She could remember so many days when her Grandpa Ben would come in from work and scoop her up in his arms, twirling her around. It always made her giggle, and she would say, "Faster, Grandpa, faster!"

Then he would come to a stop, still holding her, and say,

"Now, what has my little lassie been up to today?" He spoke with a slight Irish accent. His parents had come over from Ireland, and even though he had never lived there, he had picked up some of his pronunciations from them.

"We made gwape jelly. I helped Grandma pick the gwapes all by myself. Then Grandma put them in a big pot to cook them. After that, she put them in the big sack. She let me squish and squeeze them. It was so much fun!"

He replied with a smile, "That might explain your purple lips. I assume you tasted your creation?"

"Oh, yes," Katherine exclaimed gleefully. They were deelicious!"

* * *

Benjamin O'Riley was a tall, handsome man with thick white hair and a white mustache to match. Katherine liked the way it tickled when he would snuggle his face against her cheek. Katherine was his little shadow. She went everywhere with him. He taught her about the horses and let her help take care of them. If he was fixing a fence, he pretended to let her hammer in the nails. He would put her on his lap when he was running the tractor to cut the grass and even let her help steer it. He would also sing to her. He had the most beautiful voice.

After he put her down, he walked over to Grandma Elizabeth where she stood at the sink cleaning up the dishes. He gave her a tight, warm hug and gently kissed her on the lips.

She smiled up at him with a warm gaze. He whispered something in her ear that made her giggle a girlish giggle. She patted away at him and said: "Benjamin O'Riley, you are a very bad boy!"

Katherine, looking on, said, "Grandpa... Why do you kiss Grandma like that?"

"Well, my dear Katie, that would be because I love her so

and she's my wife. That's the way couples in love act," he replied.

"I'm going to marry Jason. I love him the bestest of all the boys," she said. "Grandpa, you should go sit in the time-out chair. Grandma said you are a very bad boy!"

Her Grandmother was an elegant woman. She was tall and slender with ash-blonde hair. She had long, slender fingers, and her skin was always so soft. She was a very polished lady and made certain that Katherine and Melanie always used good manners. Katherine loved to watch her sew. She made the cutest little dresses for both girls, and when they outgrew them, she taught them how to make a quilt using the fabric from the dresses. She wished she had remembered to bring her quilt that she had kept along the foot of her bed. She treasured it so. It somehow always brought her comfort.

Other than just with each other, the girls also spent much of their time with Jason. His family lived close by. Grandpa called them the Three Musketeers. There was so much for children to do on the acres of land. It was like being in a magical wonderland, with never-ending possibilities of using their imaginations to create wonderfully entertaining things to do. They seldom got into mischief, but when they did, it was never anything serious. However, Grandma Elizabeth would always discipline them, anyway. Jason occasionally had to go home, and Katherine and Melanie would be sent to their rooms. Grandma never sent Melanie home.

Her heart ached for the poor child. She deserved so much more than what her son and daughter-in-law gave to her. She had spoken with him countless times, but he wasn't the one in charge of their home. She had always assumed that he only married Regina because she had gotten pregnant. His wife could be very cold and controlling. She had never wanted to have children. Melanie had been a "mistake," to quote Regina. She had made sure nothing like that ever happened again. She gave her monetary things, for sure, but the child was desperate for love and attention. Benjamin and Elizabeth did whatever they could to fill the void and bring love and happiness to their other granddaughter's life.

The three children were inseparable even into their school years. They were all excellent students and would get together to do homework and work on class projects together. They were sometimes in the same classes together, but not always. They often celebrated birthday parties at the ranch, as Ben referred to it. He would give the children hayrides and set up pony rides. Grandma would let them decorate cookies, make caramel apples, and bob for apples.

As teenagers, they would often get together with a group of friends and go to the movies. One evening, after walking out of the theater in Mt. Pleasant, Jason reached out and took hold of Katherine's hand. It felt so natural yet sent a strange sensation throughout her body. They became a couple naturally, as if they were just meant to be. No one was at all surprised. They had always been together in some fashion, and the special chemistry they had could be felt just by being around them.

Katherine could not get over how handsome Jason was. He was six feet, two inches tall and had dark brown hair and green eyes. He was so loving and attentive to her. It truly baffled them both that they had not realized this kind of love for one another sooner. They knew they had always loved each other as friends growing up, but this was different. This was an all-encompassing kind of love.

Melanie dated various boys off and on but had not yet found a love connection. She was a little on the wild side. She seldom missed a party and drank way too much. Katherine felt Melanie had lost her virginity long ago. It was not surprising, considering Melanie didn't have rules or curfews to follow. Her parents didn't pay attention to what she did if they weren't bothered. She was pretty much raising herself and not doing such a good job. The only thing she was driven to do was to get good grades in school so she could go away to college.

When Melanie turned 18, she bounded out of bed and ran to the kitchen. She was pretty sure there would be some sort of surprise for her. The kitchen was empty when she entered. She looked around the room and noticed nothing out of the ordinary. She was feeling unusually happy about this birthday. Yesterday, she received her acceptance to attend the University of Virginia in the fall. Katherine had received her acceptance last week. They had both wanted to go away to the same college together. This was indeed a time for celebration.

She went about the house, calling out, "Mama, Daddy, where are you?"

"Up here, Melanie. In my bedroom."

Melanie bound up the stairs excitedly to her parent's bedroom, sure her mother must have something special for her. Dresses and various outfits were splayed out all over the bed.

"Sweetheart, I sure could use your help. Which of these would look good for me to wear when we go to the country club tonight?"

"Oh, Mama. We're going to the country club to celebrate my birthday?"

Her mother looked down at her Rolex watch with a puzzled look.

"Well, so it is. Your birthday snuck up on me. We are going to the country club with the Marshalls and the Andersons. I'm sure that would bore you to tears, darling. You'd be much better off doing something with Katherine and your friends." She walked over and picked up her purse. She took out a credit card and handed it to Melanie. "Why don't you go shopping and pick out something pretty for yourself?"

With a credit card in hand, Melanie left without saying a word to her mother and went to her room, slamming the door. She collapsed on her bed. She felt utterly deflated. How could her parents not want to celebrate her birthday with her? Even worse, how could her mother have forgotten it was her birthday? Why was she not important to her? She had never felt truly loved and cherished by her mother but didn't understand why. She was determined that if she ever became a parent, she would make sure her child felt adored. Just then, her cell phone rang. It was Kat.

"Happy Birthday, kiddo," she said happily. "What's the plan to celebrate turning eighteen?"

Melanie repeatedly turned the credit card in her fingers. A devious smile crossed her lips. "How would you like to join me on a shopping excursion, compliments of my mother?"

"Wow, that sounds awesome. What time should I pick you up?"

"I'll be ready in an hour. Love you, Kat."

"Love you more. See you soon."

Her Dad called her while she was getting ready to wish her a happy birthday and tell her he was bringing home a surprise for her. She was so excited and grateful. She told him she might be at Grandma and Grandpa's house. He told her not to worry, and he'd plan to take it to her there unless she called to let him know differently.

* * *

Eight hours and hundreds of dollars later, the girls returned to their grandparents' house. They swept Melanie in their arms with warm hugs and birthday wishes.

"You just missed your father, Melanie," her grandmother said. "He left you a special surprise and said to tell you how much he loves you." She took Melanie into the parlor, where the most beautiful cake from her favorite bakery in the world sat. It was from The Cake Stand in Charleston. He had taken the time to special order a cake. A cheerful expression came over her face.

After a wonderful dinner Grandma Elizabeth had made in Melanie's honor and opening her gifts from them and, of course, some of her special cake, the girls headed up to their bedrooms to unload the treasures they had purchased that day. They spent the rest of the night trying on their clothes, laughing, and having incredible girl time. They talked way into the wee hours until exhausted and eventually fell into their beds.

As Melanie was falling asleep, she thought to herself, *This turned out to be a great birthday after all, despite my mother.*

Chapter Six

Caps flew in the air. High school graduation day had finally arrived. Parties and celebrations were planned at various places around the entire island. Katherine and Melanie's grandparents were hosting a celebration at their house for the two of them, with family and all their friends in attendance. Even Melanie's parents had come, and Regina had helped Elizabeth plan and set up for the event.

Just before graduation, Katherine, Melanie, and Jason had made plans for leaving to go to college. The girls were so excited about getting settled in Charlottesville. The campus was lovely. It had been voted number one of the most beautiful campuses in America. It was a national historic landmark created by Thomas Jefferson in 1819. Edgar Allan Poe had attended before being thrown out for cheating, and his dorm room was still on display for visitors. One of their favorite places on the campus was the Rotunda, which served as the heart of the university. There was a long, lush green lawn with pavilions on the eastern and western sides, flanking living quarters for the most honored students. Only the very best were offered quarters on "the lawn.". Katherine was enrolled in the five-year MBA program in English education, and Melanie was attending the Curry School at Ruffner Hall to get her B.S. ED/M. Ed in kinesiology. She wanted a career in physical therapy for sports medicine.

Jason had received an appointment to the Naval Academy in Annapolis. He desperately wanted to become an officer in the Marines. Unfortunately, you don't get to pick whether they assign you to the Navy or the Marines. The academy chooses upon graduation, and you have no choice. They chose only around 20 percent to be Marines, and the rest became Navy. He had to report on June 28th for Induction and Plebe summer. Those seven weeks were required for all incoming freshmen and were comprised of rigorous physical and mental training. It would be exhausting and frantic as the new incoming midshipmen were broken down and shaped to develop the qualities of a naval officer.

The month of June flew by. Katherine, Jason, Melanie, and a group of their friends had rented a house in Myrtle Beach on the Golden Mile after graduation. They spent their days on the beach lounging, swimming, and playing volleyball and cornhole. They spent their nights going out to the many fun restaurants in the area, like Pier 14 on the ocean and Margaritaville at Broadway on the beach.

Jason had to report to the Naval Academy in a couple of weeks to start Plebes. The closer they got to the date, the stranger he acted. Katherine couldn't quite find the right words to describe it. He wasn't acting distant– maybe just more serious and somewhat withdrawn at times, as though he was lost in thought. She often wondered if he was second-guessing his decision to go to the Academy. When she would ask him about it, he'd just say, "Everything's fine, Kat. You don't need to worry about me."

He and Katherine went to Annapolis a few days early to have time alone together. It would surely be quite some time before they would see each other again. They stayed at the Annapolitan Bed & Breakfast on West Street, close to the Academy. It was an elegant, restored farmhouse dating back to 1870. Beautiful grounds surrounded the house, which possessed a wrap-around porch. The entranceway was majestic, with a long crystal chandelier hanging from the tall ceiling just before the lovely historic staircase. Their room was decorated in a nautical theme, with a private bath and a separate sitting area. A three-course breakfast would be available every morning in the ornate dining room or on a terrace.

They left very early that morning for the eight-hour drive to Annapolis. After they had gotten settled into their room, Jason suggested they go jogging on the grounds of the Academy. The campus was beautiful. They went past Bancroft Hall, with its amazing architecture, and stopped briefly at the chapel. They were both in awe and unable to speak. It was one of the most beautiful buildings either of them had ever seen. A place that could hardly be captured in pictures but must be seen in person to appreciate its beauty. They found their way to the path that led to the waterfront where the sailboats were and stopped for a spell. They sat and rested on a stone bench. The view was beautiful and peaceful.

Jason had grown increasingly quiet during their jog, and it gave Katherine an uncomfortable feeling. After they had rested for a couple of minutes, Jason turned to her and said, "Kat, I need to talk to you about something." She looked into his eyes and did not know what she saw there. All she knew was that she had never seen a look like that on his face before. "What is it, Jason? You're scaring me." It took what seemed like forever before he spoke.

"Kat, we both have an endless road ahead of us and a lot to

accomplish. We will not be able to see each other much. Life's going to be a lot different for both of us."

Of course, she already knew that, but couples did this type of thing all the time. "Jason, you don't need to tell me that. I already know it's going to be different. We'll make the best of the time we can carve out to be together."

"Kat, what I'm trying to say to you is that I don't want you to be my girlfriend anymore."

Before he could go on, Katherine's lip trembled, and her eyes swelled up with tears. She felt her heart shattering into pieces. Talking through her tears and quivering voice, she said, "Jason, please don't do this. We can figure it out. We'll be just fine. We have a lifetime of memories together. I love you so much, Jason. Please don't break up with me."

He dropped to his knee in front of her, cupped her face in his hands, and said, "Shhhh.... Katherine, listen to me. I'm not finished. We just can't go on being boyfriend and girlfriend." He reached into his pants pocket, pulled out a small, blue velvet box, and opened it to reveal a pear-shaped diamond ring. When the time is right for us, I want you to be my wife. Will you marry me, Katherine?"

She brought her hands up to her face and started sobbing. Jason reached for her hands, saying, "Katherine, is that a yes?"

She could hardly speak. She looked down at him with an enormous grin on her tear-stained face and said, "Yes, yes, Jason, I will marry you." She jumped into his arms and wrapped her legs around his waist. As he gently spun her around, they kissed the most heavenly kiss—a kiss that would keep them connected forever.

After a magical time in bed making passionate love, Jason told her they needed to get changed for dinner. She laid her head on his shoulder, wrapped her arms around him, and said, "How can you think of food at a time like this? I'm not even hungry. You're all I want."

He chuckled as he peeled himself out of her arms, saying, "Woman, I am ravenous. You've worked off everything I've eaten today." He reached over, popped her behind, and said, "Now, get up and wear something dressy."

Reluctantly, she complied, saying as she was climbing out of bed, "Where are we going, anyway?"

He pulled her into his arms once more and said, "That, future Mrs. Jason Kelly, is a surprise."

Jason had made reservations beforehand at O'Leary's Seafood, an upscale old house with an intimate setting. He had made the entire staff aware of the reason behind this dinner. When they entered the restaurant, the hostess greeted them and said, "This must be the future Mr. & Mrs. Kelly, I presume?"

Katherine's mouth spread into a gigantic smile, and Jason replied, "You would be correct. Thank You."

They were seated at a very private table. The surroundings were very cozy, and the staff knew of their engagement and bothered them only when necessary. The evening and dinner had been magical. To Katherine, this felt like a dream, a fairy tale.

Jason paid the check, and they thanked the staff profusely for helping to make their evening so special. They all seemed genuinely happy for the couple and wished them the best and congratulations.

They ambled back to the Inn arm in arm. Neither of them had ever felt so happy.

During the precious days that followed, they spent time exploring Annapolis. Historic Annapolis took up half of one of their days. It had plenty of shops, boutiques, and places to eat.

They took a sailboat out on the bay one leisurely afternoon with a basket filled with wine, cheeses, crackers, and various meat selections.

They visited the Harewood House and the Banneker-Douglass Museum and toured more of the Academy.

They spent their last day together at Quiet Waters Park. It was picturesque, with a six-mile paved path perfect for strolling along and taking in the beauty. They made their way to the park's south river to see the panoramic view and rented kayaks to take out on the water. They thoroughly enjoyed seeing the sculpture garden, especially Katherine, who loved to garden herself.

As they prepared to head back to the Inn, sadness overcame them both. During the past few days, they had committed themselves to each other for the rest of their lives. That they were not married yet had no relevance. Their souls were already united.

Chapter Seven

Induction day was finally here. They tearfully said their goodbyes, and then Jason reported to the Academy to join the 1,100 others waiting for processing. They would give up all their possessions: cell phones, clothes, shoes, long hair, and even underwear. They would be issued everything they needed for their existence, down to their shampoo. Katherine would have no contact with him for the next forty-four days.

She had stayed in Annapolis to attend the ceremony. Even though there were tears in her eyes, she did not feel sad. She was so thrilled and proud of Jason. He was pursuing his dream. She was looking at a future officer of the Navy or Marines. She was also looking at her future husband. The pride she felt was overwhelming. She knew she would miss him, and there would be many times they would have to spend apart, but she also knew that nothing could break the bond they shared, and they could withstand any challenge.

The drive home was quite peaceful. The sun was beginning to set as she pulled down the lane to park her car. Her grandma and grandpa were sitting in the rockers on the porch, sipping iced tea. When they saw her, they both got up with arms outstretched to welcome her home. After Grandma hugged her, she pulled back and took Katherine's left hand in hers while excitedly saying, "Let me see the ring.".

"Grandma, you knew?"

Ben spoke up and said, "Of course, we knew. I'm not about to give my dear Katie away to anyone who does not ask me for your hand in marriage properly."

He was smiling from ear to ear as he reached out and took her in his arms for a warm hug.

Katherine was stunned and impressed with Jason because she knew her grandparents would prefer that he propose properly. She had never been so happy in her life. She slept well that night and had sweet dreams of her life with Jason.

She met Melanie for lunch the next day at Poe's Tavern. Like her grandma, Melanie grabbed her left hand, saying excitedly, "Let me see that thing. Oh, Kat, it's exquisite. I'm so happy for you. You and Jason were meant to be together."

"I'm so happy, Mel. It's like I'm living in a fairy tale. The love I have for Jason runs so deep. I can't imagine my life without him and wouldn't want to."

They talked nonstop over lunch about their excitement for the future. They would leave at the end of the month for college and had a lot to do before then. They already knew they would room together. As first-year students, they were required to live in the dorms, but they didn't mind. Neither of them would have wanted it any other way.

Melanie's father, Dan, rented a van to pack everything they would need to take with them. They had a small convoy going to Charlottesville. Melanie and her mother were in Melanie's car, Katherine and Elizabeth were in her car, and Ben rode with Dan in the van. It only took about five hours to get there, and everyone was in great spirits. It was a beautiful place, and you could feel the excitement in the air. Their life at UVA had finally begun.

Their college years flew by. Katherine and Jason had limited time to spend together but took advantage whenever he got leave. Academics were vigorous for all three of them, but they were committed to doing the very best they could.

At the start of their fourth year, Melanie came rushing into the apartment they had moved into after their first year. "Kat, you will not believe this. I have met the most amazing guy. His name is Chris Sandston, and he's getting his degree in sports medicine as an athletic trainer. We have so much in common. I think he may be the one."

Laughing, Kat said, "Mel, take a breath. I think this is wonderful. When can I meet him?"

"We're meeting at the pedestrian mall for lunch. Please come too. I want you to meet him. I know you're going to like him."

Katherine met Chris, and they hit it off right away. Like Melanie, she felt that he was probably the one.

The threesome went to Annapolis over a weekend to introduce Chris to Jason. As Katherine knew would happen, the guys connected immediately. It was as if the four of them had been together for years. While the girls went shopping, the guys went to play golf. They were always joking when they got back about who would beat whom the next time. One weekend, they went up to Annapolis for a football game. When Katherine saw the midshipmen march onto the field, her heart warmed with the most profound amount of pride she had ever felt in her entire life. Jason and the other future officers were filing onto the football field, standing and facing the cheering crowd. The game had been exceptionally exciting. With only three seconds to go, the midshipmen scored a touchdown, winning the game.

* * *

It was graduation day for Jason. Katherine, Melanie, Chris, and Jason's parents sat in the stands of the Navy-Marine Corps Memorial Stadium, watching as the graduating class marched in, two by two, with their hats tucked under their left arms. Jason still had not told Katherine whether he was an Ensign in the Navy or a 2nd lieutenant in the Marines. As they marched in, she suddenly saw Jason in his Marine uniform marching proudly. She grabbed Melanie's arm and said excitedly, "Mel, look, there's Jason. He's a Marine, just as he dreamed of."

Melanie yelled, "Way to go, Jason," and embraced Katherine tightly.

Once they had all filed in, the Navy-Blue Angels did a fly over the stadium. That was indeed a sight to see. Dignitaries gave several speeches and comments, and then the Secretary of the Navy asked the graduating class to stand as he read the oath of office. In the end, the graduates said in unison, "I Do." Upon receiving their diplomas, the newly commissioned Ensigns and 2nd Lieutenants stood and sang the Blue and Gold. They then tossed their hats in the air, and the crowd cheered. Children rushed down to the field to grab the hats, and family and friends filed down to mingle and find their graduates. Katherine and the others finally found Jason shaking hands with other graduates.

When Katherine spotted him, she shouted, "Jason, Jason!"

He turned and saw her and immediately started running toward her. He scooped her into his arms and said, "Beautiful, I'm a second Lieutenant in the Marines." Tears streamed down Katherine's face as she said, "Jason, I am so very proud of you and happy that you are going to fulfill your dream."

"I have even more news, Kat. After my leave, they selected me to go to Officer Candidate School in Quantico. I'm going to be an Infantry Officer. After that, I'll find out where I'll be stationed. It's happening, Kat. Everything I've ever dreamed of is coming true. You as my wife, and a Marine Officer. My life couldn't possibly be any better."

Both of their futures were coming together as each of them had planned. They both looked forward to the day they would begin their magical life together.

Chapter Eight

They planned to get married in October following Katherine's graduation from UVA. Chris and Melanie had gotten engaged the summer after Jason's graduation and were planning their wedding for June, following Melanie's graduation from UVA in May.

Following their first year at UVA, the girls found an apartment near campus where they could share. It was a townhouse with a full kitchen, family room, bedroom, and bath on the first floor. There was a lovely patio off the kitchen, so they could sit outside and watch the ducks on a small pond or grill something to eat when the guys were over. On the second floor was another bedroom with a private bath and an open loft just off the bedroom. They both agreed that the upstairs would be better for Melanie when Chris often stayed over. The downstairs space was perfect for the weekends. Jason was off and able to drive up from Camp Lejeune.

Katherine had been in her bedroom studying all weekend for finals. They would both be graduating in just a couple of weeks. She took a break and went into the kitchen to make herself a cup of tea. Melanie sat in her sweats and t-shirt with her feet crossed and propped up on the table. She held an apple and a bridal magazine in one hand.

She set her cup on the table to steep and sat across from Melanie.

"How on earth do you do it, Mel? You're planning your wedding and getting ready for finals all at the same time. I'd be a basket case if I even considered doing that."

"There isn't all that much for me to do. You know my mother. Only the best will be good enough. She has to keep up appearances for all her snooty friends. She will want to invite everybody who is anybody to my wedding. The opinions of others have always been very important to her. You, of all people, know that. It's just a shame that what they see isn't real. The only thing I told her was to run everything by me first. The final decision is mine and mine only. Plus, Lowndes Grove Plantation will handle all the details for the ceremony and reception based on what I told them. I already have my dress and shoes, so what's left is just some minor stuff."

"I mailed the invitations for your shower. That's in a couple of weeks. Regarding my wedding, I've sent out the save-the-dates and secured the Sullivan's Island Baptist Chapel. The rest will have to wait; however, it will be nothing remotely close to your wedding. The reception will be on the grounds of Gram & Grandpa's house amongst her lovely gardens. I think it's what I've always dreamed of. Speaking of Gram, have you talked to her recently?"

"Yes, Kat, and her health seems to be declining rapidly. I think she's in stage 5 now. It's only a matter of time."

"I know. I drove down to see her a couple of weeks ago when you and Chris had gone away for the weekend. She's lost a lot of weight, and her color is bad, but she is still her chipper self and has her sense of humor. She informed me she has decided that she is not ready to die and has informed God of that, too."

Giggling, Mel said, "You know, it wouldn't surprise me if she got her way. You and I both know that everyone listens to Gram, and I suspect she has God's ear, too."

"All we can do is hope for the best and cherish her while we have her. Say, are you hungry? You can't make a meal from that apple you're munching on."

"I'm famished, Kat, but I couldn't find anything to eat."

She smiled at her cousin and said, "You mean you couldn't find anything you felt like cooking. She looked in the refrigerator and said, "How about I whip up a couple of omelets? We've got some spinach, mushrooms, cheese, and eggs."

"Whew, girl. That sounds incredible. Most people would just throw some toast in the toaster, but not you– you throw together a gourmet meal in a matter of minutes. You should have been a chef with your cooking skills."

"It's always been something I love to do. Cooking alongside Gram all those years when I was growing up was such a big part of my life and such a sense of enjoyment. Now, it's more of a passion and even a release from my day's pressures. That and I truly love cooking for others."

"You know, Kat, you have such strong nurturing skills. It feels like you've always taken care of all of us, even growing up. We'd be running around and probably up to no good, and you'd be inside baking cookies. You're going to be a great mom one day."

"Thanks, Mel. I want lots of children."

After they ate their omelets, they took advantage of the beautiful spring day and took a walk. The town was bubbling with tourists. Charlottesville was always that way, especially when the weather was nice. The campus was as exceptional to see as it was to go there. You could feel its historical value and its prestige. While they were both somewhat saddened to leave, they also looked forward to the next chapter in their lives.

* * *

Melanie's wedding was as glamorous as they both knew it would be. Her gown was an Oscar de la Renta. It probably cost more than Katherine planned to spend on her entire wedding, but Melanie looked absolutely lovely. Her grandmother had given her the pearl earrings she had worn at her wedding for Melanie to use as something old, but she also cherished the fact that she was giving them to one of her beloved granddaughters.

Regina, as Melanie predicted, had invited more than three hundred people. Melanie and Chris didn't even know half of them. They decorated the reception hall elaborately enough for a royal wedding. The guests had been asked to respond to the formal invitation with their dinner selection, which waiters would serve in formal attire. Even the invitations must have cost a fortune. Card stock was not acceptable to Regina O'Reilly. Melanie and Chris had selected the DJ for the wedding reception. She and Chris had chosen a lovely slow song to begin their dance together. Regina smiled regally, nodding at the other guests with apparent pride. During a pause in the music, they suddenly sprung into the song from Dirty Dancing. The guests broke out in cheers and whistles. Melanie even separated from Chris and vaulted into his arms, at which point he raised her above his head, just like in the movie. Wild applause could be heard throughout the reception hall, and everyone was on their feet. After that, the bridal party joined to finish the dance with them. The entire group had practiced this. It was perfectly choreographed. When the dance was over, Melanie, somewhat winded, had an enormous smile as she gazed around the room at the guests. Her eyes fell upon her mother standing at her table. The expression on her face resembled that of a disapproving nun.

Melanie shrugged it off, refusing to let anything spoil this day. The next dance was the bride's dance with her father. Melanie had chosen the song because the lyrics had a special meaning to her from when she was young. She had chosen "Butterfly Kisses." Her daddy had tears streaming down his face as they danced.

"I love you, Kitten."

"I love you too, Daddy." It was a moment they would both cherish forever.

They danced the night away. When it was time to leave, the guests were waiting outside in two lines, and all held sparklers as Melanie and Chris made their way to their awaiting white limo.

They had already started looking for a place to live before their wedding and had settled on a cute little cap cod in Mt. Pleasant that the owner had agreed to rent to them for now, with an option to purchase later.

* * *

It was a beautiful October day. Katherine could not believe she would finally marry Jason, the love of her life whom she had met as a kid. What were the odds of that?

Katherine and her bridesmaids were in her room, getting ready for the blessed event. The atmosphere was joyful, with lots of talking and laughter. Melanie, of course, was her matron of honor. The girls helped her get into her relatively simple gown, which had a full chiffon skirt that swished when she moved and a short train. The top had a V-neck with capped sleeves that fell off her shoulders. Her grandmother walked into the room, and tears formed in her eyes when she looked at Katherine.

"You look so exquisite, my precious Katie. I am so happy for you but will surely miss my little girl."

Katherine walked over, wrapped her arms around her grandmother, and embraced her in a warm hug.

"Grandma, I won't be far away and will be here whenever you need me."

She, too, had tears in her eyes because she knew her grandmother's health was failing, and she would not have her much longer. When they pulled away from each other, her grandmother handed Katherine a small white velvet box. She gave it to Katherine.

"My mother gave this to me on the day I got married. I've been saving it for you." Katherine opened the box, revealing the most beautiful oval-shaped locket surrounded by tiny diamonds. The inside was scripted with the words "I'll love you forever."

"Oh, Grandma, this is so incredibly beautiful. I'll wear it today and cherish it forever."

It was time to get to the church. Katherine had splurged on a stretch limo to take her and the bridesmaids. She felt giddy with excitement and like her heart might jump out of her chest.

They had had their ceremony at Sullivan's Island Baptist Church. It was quaint and non-assuming. Just what they both wanted. They decorated the church's pulpit with ferns and candles, while the pews were decorated with primroses, baby's breath, and lithe greenery secured with a white ribbon.

She took her grandfather's arm to walk down the aisle. Jason was waiting at the front of the church with his groomsmen and the pastor. He was wearing his dress blues and looked so incredibly handsome. He reached up and wiped a tiny tear falling down her cheek. They said their vows and exchanged their rings.

The pastor said, "By the authority vested in me by the state of South Carolina, I now pronounce you husband and wife.

What God has joined together, let no man put asunder. You may kiss your bride." He then instructed them to turn and face those who witnessed their marriage. "Ladies and Gentlemen, I present to you for the first time Mr. & Mrs. Jason Douglas Kelly." The congregation lit up in applause and cheers.

As they exited the church after the ceremony, eight Marines from Jason's platoon formed an arch of raised, tilted sabers for them to walk through.

A horse-drawn white carriage pulled by Katherine's horse, Lucky, took them from the church. It was a brief ride, but they had diligently ensured he had been appropriately walked and exercised before this day. Their reception was at her grandparents' ranch. They had ordered a large white tent capable of setting up tables for dining for up to one hundred people. It had sheer white panels hanging down from the vaulted top that could be left open or closed; they were gathered at intervals all the way around and were tied with navy blue ribbons to match the bridesmaids' dresses. They had set the tables with white tablecloths, place settings, and glasses. Each table had an enormous arrangement of candles and begonias from her grandmother's garden. The ceiling had been draped with lights. They hired a small staff member to collect plates and glasses as the guests finished with them. The dance floor was in the tent's center and was visible to everyone. Katherine and Jason used the same DJ that Melanie and Chris used because they liked him so much.

The DJ announced the entire bridal party as they entered the tent's opening. Jason's parents first followed her grandparents, groomsmen escorted the bridesmaids, and then the DJ announced she and Jason. Applause filled the air, and Katherine felt like she was floating on it. The smile on her face felt like it might freeze there.

Jason led her to the center of the dance floor, where they danced to "Perfect." It was as though the song was written for them. They glided along the dance floor as if they were in their own little world and nobody was there.

"I feel like Cinderella, Jason."

"You're more beautiful than Cinderella. I can't believe you're mine."

After their dance, they joined their guests, helping themselves with drinks and appetizers. Katherine had elected to have stations around the reception tent's outer perimeter instead of the more formal option of asking guests to make dinner selections when replying to their invitations. There was an area for the bar, an area with tiered fruits, an assortment of appetizers, and an area where dinner would be. They both wanted their reception to be a comfortable, casual event that would feel more like a family gathering.

Ben tapped his glass and asked for everyone's attention. "As I look at my granddaughter, Katherine, I can't help but reflect on all the years I was lucky enough to watch her grow and become the beautiful woman she is today. She captured my heart on the day she was born, and I became increasingly in awe of her as the years passed. She's my princess and my ray of sunlight; no matter her age, she'll always be those things to me. But today, as I watch her marry a wonderful man, I'm filled with pride and am confident that she and Jason are about to embark on a wonderful journey filled with the love and happiness that can only come as man and wife. May the two of you always treat each other with love, compassion, and respect. Please join me today in congratulating the bride and groom and wishing them all the best for a long and happy life together."

The DJ then asked everyone to take their seats as the bride would like to dance with her grandfather. Katherine had chosen "Have I Told You Lately That I Love You?" Tears formed in her eyes as they danced. They needed no words between them. She cherished every memory of being raised by her grandparents and would use all she had learned growing up to be a loving wife to Jason and, eventually, a good mother to their children.

Their reception lasted nearly four hours. No one was in any hurry to leave, and the magic in the atmosphere swept away Katherine and Jason. Upon Jason's instruction, the DJ announced that the next song would be the last dance before the bride and groom departed.

Their guests had arranged themselves in two rows just outside the tent opening and tossed wedding birdseed instead of swirling sparklers as had been done at Melanie and Chris's wedding. After all, this land was full of nature, so indeed, one of God's creatures would enjoy it. They spent their first night at the Ansonborough Inn in Charleston, a charming boutique hotel. From there, they went to Charlottesville to visit some vineyards and then to Camp Lejeune, North Carolina, where Jason was stationed. Katherine's things had already been shipped to their house, except for the few things she had known she would need in the meantime.

Their journey together had finally begun.

Chapter Nine

Katherine loved their life at Camp Lejeune. Remembering the first day they had gotten to their house after their honeymoon brought a smile to her face. When they had pulled into the driveway, her hands had flown to her cheeks, and she had squealed with delight as though she was a child on Christmas morning. She jumped out of the car and raced up to the front door with excitement to go in.

As she put her key in the door, she heard Jason say, "Not so fast, beautiful." He was running up so fast she felt as if he might not be able to stop and would knock her over. Scooping her up with one arm under her knees and the other around her back, he kissed her and said, "I believe it's customary for the groom to carry his bride over the threshold, isn't it?"

Katherine could not help but giggle and wrapped her arms around his neck.

Their house was two stories and had a ground-level covered front porch big enough for two rocking chairs. They entered the foyer with a beautiful arched opening leading into the dining room. There was a small room on the right that could be a sitting room or office. As they passed further down the hallway, the stairway leading to the bedrooms was on her left, just across from the large kitchen, which made her face light up. Preparing fabulous meals for her husband would be a joy. There was a long island in the room with bar stools separating the kitchen from the family room. The two spaces flowed together, so when they had friends over, there would be plenty of room to spread out without being separated. One of her favorite features of their home, though, was the screened porch off the family room that overlooked a wonderful fenced-in yard. The fence was five feet tall and constructed of white wood. She envisioned planting lots of flowers, herbs, and roses and watching their children play. It all felt too good to be true.

During their first two years of marriage, Katherine decided not to go after her Ph.D. right away. She decided instead to tutor. Many of the Marines were taking online courses to work toward a degree. She listed her service in the monthly newsletter. The calls came flooding in. They set lesson times up at the business center. When they would try to pay her, she refused to accept it. It was the least she could do to give back to those sacrificing so much for our country. So many of these young men were single, away from home, and lonely. If time permitted, they would often sit and talk after the lesson. They were so hungry for family, and her heart just broke for them. The more time she spent with them, the more attached she became to them and them to her. In some ways, even though they were not so many years younger than she was, she could offer the nurturing they so needed. They came to value her opinion, advice, and compassion. It filled her heart with joy.

One Saturday morning, Katherine rolled over in bed and just watched Jason sleep. Oh, how she loved this man. She snuggled up close to him and wrapped her arms around him. When he woke up, he kissed the top of her head as he enclosed his arms around her.

"Good morning, beautiful."

"Why don't we just stay here like this all day?" Katherine said as she snuggled up closer.

"We can't because somebody signed us up to work the Fall Festival, and I can't possibly eat all of those cupcakes that are on our kitchen counter."

"I know, but the children love the Halloween festivities. One day, we will watch our children taking part in them."

"Then I guess we need to get ourselves out of bed and get ready, but first, I'm going to make love to my wife."

Chris and Melanie came up often. It was only about a four-hour drive from where they had settled in Mount Pleasant outside of Charleston. Both couples were happy and very close. They came up when Jason was returning from his first deployment. He had been gone for eight months. Katherine, Melanie, and Chris created a massive banner that said, "Welcome home, Captain Kelly," and placed it along the highway leading to the base with hundreds of others. The weekend was fun and crazy all at the same time. Katherine had stocked up on an outrageous amount of food so she could make all his favorite dishes. When the group was sitting and eating her chicken cordon bleu, homemade biscuits, twice-baked potatoes, and spinach salad with fresh strawberries, Jason moaned in pure pleasure when he put it in his mouth.

"Babe, no other person on the face of the earth can cook like you do. I dreamed of your cooking." He leaned over and kissed her.

Melanie, poking down at the food on her plate with her fork in her hand, spoke up, saying, "Okay now, this is the gene I didn't get. I wouldn't know how to cook like this, and I'd burn down the kitchen trying." Everyone roared with laughter.

Chris put his arm around Melanie's shoulder and said, "It's okay, honey. I just love your microwaved dinners."

Melanie smacked at him. "I'm not *that* bad. I can cook simple things."

On Saturday morning, they were all cleaning up after breakfast. Melanie looked out the kitchen window above the sink, where she was rinsing off the plates, noticing what a beautiful day it was. "Hey, y'all, why don't we go to the beach?"

The others looked at each other and sprang into action.

"I'll make us some lunch," Katherine said.

"I'll grab the chairs," Jason said.

"I'll help you, Jason," Chris said.

Before they knew it, they were all packed up and on their way. After they got everything set up, Jason and Katherine took a walk. They were walking away arm in arm. Chris was rubbing sunscreen on Melanie's back. She was watching Jason and Katherine in awe.

"Look at them, Chris. You'd never know from looking at them they have been together for so many years. Their love still looks so new."

"Yes, it does, but we're like that too, aren't we?"

"Yeah, I guess so."

The girls lounged in chairs while the guys either played cornhole or joined in a game of volleyball with some others at the beach.

"What is that man thing they do, running up to each other, bumping their chests when they win at something?" Katherine said.

Melanie was laughing. "They look like the ape reinvented."

Sunday morning, Melanie found Katherine rocking in a rocking chair on the screened porch, having her cup of tea. She looked like she was a million miles away, lost in thought. She curled up in the rocker next to Katherine.

"Good morning. Earth to Katherine."

Katherine didn't turn her head but smiled. "Morning, Mel."

"What are you so lost in thought about?"

"I've just been sitting here looking at my roses and thinking of Grandma. I miss her so much."

"So do I. I'm just so glad she did not have to suffer any longer."

"It's hard to believe she's been gone for six months, Mel. I remember Grandpa calling to tell me she had died in her sleep like it was yesterday. Her service was beautiful. I loved the way Grandpa had filled the chapel with roses."

"As painful as it was to lose her, Kat, it was also a time to be together, heal, and talk about our wonderful memories of her. I have my pearl earrings, and you'll always have your locket to keep her close to you. I notice every time I see you, you're wearing it. Do you ever take it off?"

"Only when I shower. It's something I hold very dear to my heart, along with her apron that Grandpa let me have." Her head was still resting back against the rocker. She turned it toward Melanie, looking at her for the first time since they began reminiscing. "You're looking a little pale this morning. Are you feeling okay?"

"I feel a little under the weather. I'm a little nauseous and exhausted. It may be just from drinking way too much wine this weekend, not to mention eating your fabulous cooking. I've eaten way more than I'm used to eating over the past couple of days. My body's in shock." She gave out a small chuckle.

"You do look a little tired. Maybe you were in the sun too long yesterday. Would you like me to make you some toast or something? It might help to make you feel better."

"That sounds like a good idea, Kat. Thanks."

Katherine got up from her rocker and went into the house.

As she stood up and started to go into the house behind Katherine, Melanie began to wobble and grabbed hold of the door frame to gain her balance. Before she had walked more than two steps, she passed out, falling hard on the floor.

Katherine, hearing the noise, ran into the family room and found Melanie sprawled out, unconscious. She said her name several times but got no response. She started yelling for Chris and Jason, who were still upstairs. Chris was the first to come barreling down with no shirt on and just his shorts, followed by Jason. He slid down on his knees next to where Melanie was lying with Katherine by her side.

"What happened, Kat?"

"I don't know, Chris. She said she was feeling a little under the weather and tired, so I went to make her something to eat, hoping it would make her feel better, and then I heard a loud noise and found her passed out."

Melanie started coming around but was still very much in a foggy state.

"What happened?" she asked, looking up at Chris.

"You passed out, baby. We should take you to see a doctor."

"There is no need for that. I'm just feeling a little tired, is all, and a little queasy. It's nothing that a little rest won't cure."

"You're probably right, but I don't think we should take any chances before we get in the car this afternoon for the drive home." He was worried. Melanie never got sick, but she looked horrible to him.

He helped her get into the car, putting on his shirt and shoes almost simultaneously.

They went to a medical center just down the road from the main entrance of the base. Chris went back with Melanie while Katherine and Jason waited in the lobby. The wait seemed to last forever. Katherine was pacing and wringing her hands.

Melanie was on the exam table, and Chris was stroking her head. The doctor examined her and asked her a lot of questions about her family history.

"You might have picked up the flu bug that's been going around. I'll run a couple of tests; it shouldn't take too long," the doctor said.

When the Doctor reentered the room, Melanie eased herself up to a sitting position. "Melanie, how long have you been feeling like this?"

"I've felt fine until this morning, although I have been a little tired lately."

He smiled at her. "It's nothing serious, but the bad news is that you may feel this way for a while. You are pregnant, Melanie."

Melanie and Chris could not believe their ears. They both looked stunned.

"But I've been taking the pill. Won't that hurt the baby?"

"This kind of thing happens sometimes. Birth control is not always one hundred percent effective. Everything should be fine, but I encourage you to make an appointment with your gynecologist. I don't see any need to keep you any longer. Congratulations to you both."

After he left the room, Melanie put her hands on her tummy and looked at Chris, smiling. "Chris, we are going to have a baby."

He put his arms around her, hugging her tightly. They both had enormous smiles on their faces.

She pulled back and said to him, "I can't believe this, honey. How did this happen?"

"Do I need to review the facts of life with you, my dear?" Chris said.

Melanie laughed. "Let's go tell Kat and Jason the good news."

Katherine was the first to see them walking out and immediately started running to Melanie, with Jason right behind her.

"Mel, are you okay? You were back there for a long time."

Melanie looked at Chris and then back at Katherine with a smile on her face.

"Okay, you two, you look like the cat that ate the canary. What's up?"

"I hope you're ready to be an aunt because I'm pregnant, Kat."

Katherine shrieked in delight. She threw her arms around Melanie, saying, "That is incredible news. We will have so much fun shopping and decorating your nursery. I can't wait to plan your baby shower. Have you told your parents yet? How far along are you? When are you due?"

Melanie was laughing hysterically now. "Slow down, Kat. We only just found out ourselves. You're the first to know. We'll know more once I see my OB. Wow, I didn't think I'd be hearing those words out of my mouth so soon."

"So, you guys weren't trying?"

"Nope. It's as big a surprise to us as it is to you."

At that point, Jason, who had already congratulated Chris, wrapped his arms around Melanie, giving her a warm hug. "Well, Little Mama, it looks like your life is about to change. You will be a great mom."

* * *

Later that afternoon, Chris and Melanie needed to get back home for work on Monday. Katherine gave Melanie a long, warm hug and made her promise to call and give her the details about the baby as soon as she got them.

Jason and Katherine stayed on the porch, waving goodbye before going inside.

"Can you believe this, Jason? We are going to be an aunt and uncle. The next few months will be very exciting."

"They are. It got me thinking, though. Why don't we try? It would be nice if Melanie and Chris's child and ours could be close in age and grow up together as you and Melanie did."

"That would be nice, and I'd like that. I think we should wait for a little while because you're leaving in January for six months, and I don't want to have the baby while you're gone."

"That makes sense. Why don't we start trying in November? You'll get pregnant before I leave, and the baby will be due sometime next summer."

They both agreed to make it a plan. Life had taken a dramatic turn in the last couple of days. First, Melanie found out she would have a baby, and then Katherine and Jason decided to start a family of their own.

Chapter Ten

Melanie called Katherine later the following week to fill her in on the details. Her doctor's appointment had gone well, and she was due at the end of April. Chris had gone with her. The doctor did not appear to have any concerns that she had gotten pregnant while on the pill. He reassured her and said, as with all pregnancies, they would do tests along the way.

Katherine did not tell her she and Jason were going to try soon. This was Melanie's time, and she did not want to steal her thunder. They talked instead about how joyous the next few months were going to be.

"It still hasn't sunk in, Kat. I'm going to be a Mother, and I wasn't even sure I wanted children until now. I'd assumed you'd have several children, with your strong nurturing instincts, by the time I had any at all. I'm frightened, Kat. I mean, what if I don't have what it takes? I didn't exactly have an excellent example of how to be a Leave-It-To-Beaver mother growing up if you get what I mean. What if I end up being just like her?"

"You're not your mother. You have a warm heart and care

deeply about people. You wouldn't have it in you to be disengaged like your mother was."

"You mean *is*, don't you? I called her the other day to tell her I was pregnant, and the only thing she said was, 'Oh, that's lovely, darling.' There wasn't any of the excitement or giddiness in her voice that I expected to hear– or, better said, wished to hear. What's it going to take for my mother to love and be proud of me? I've felt she was sorry my entire life that she had me."

"You and I both know it has nothing to do with you. Children learn what they live, and her mother, your grandmother, was about as cold as ice from what we've been told. You will be different. You are different. Most importantly, you will break the cycle for all future generations of Sandstons. Now, let's talk about the fun stuff. We're coming down for Thanksgiving. This will be our first one without Gram, so I'm going to make a massive feast just like she used to do. I think that's what she would have wanted. We'll be there through the weekend, so maybe you and I can start making plans for what you want your nursery to look like. "

"What a fabulous idea. Leave it to you to come up with the perfect plan. I wish I were as organized as you, but that's never been one of my strong points. I'm going to need all the help I can get."

"It's going to be so much fun, and I can sew a lot of things you might need to cut down on cost. We'll do it slowly, depending on how you're feeling. By the way, how are you feeling?"

"I'm actually feeling pretty good. My doctor told me to eat lots of high-carb foods like pasta, cereal, toast, and potatoes, sip on fruit juice or water, and, most of all, get plenty of rest and fresh air. I think all the drinking and probably eating things I shouldn't have eaten last weekend took its toll on me. I'm much better now."

"That's awesome. I'm so glad. We were all so worried about you, but everything turned out better than fine."

They hung up, promising to call each other again soon. A week did not go by that they didn't talk. Melanie was not only like a sister but also her best friend. Katherine cherished their relationship, and she knew Melanie felt the same way.

By the time Katherine saw Melanie again in November, she looked pregnant. She had such a small frame; it didn't take much for that baby bump to show. She was waiting at Grandpa's estate when they got there. Ben and Melanie were both sitting on the back porch rocking in the rockers and got up upon seeing them and met them halfway across the lawn. She hugged her grandpa tightly. He looked a little older and possibly frailer, but she was certain he was still mourning the loss of Elizabeth. Then she hugged Melanie, which Jason had already done, telling her how good she looked. "You are simply glowing, Mel. Pregnancy agrees with you," he had said.

"I'm so happy to see you guys. Chris and I are so excited we can't stand it, but we can't decide whether we want to know the baby's gender ahead of time or wait for it to be a surprise. What are your thoughts on that?"

"What my thoughts are is that it is a decision for you and Chris to make and none of my business." They both laughed as they walked arm-in-arm toward the house while Jason unloaded their things from the car and took them up to Katherine's old bedroom.

Katherine had written up the menu before she and Jason left Jacksonville for the drive down on Tuesday. They would go to the store in the morning to get what she needed after she had inventoried the kitchen to see what might be there already. She would start cooking later in the afternoon on Wednesday and most of the day on Thanksgiving day, but it would be a labor of love. She had packed her grandma's apron to wear while she prepared their meal. Thinking of that put a smile on her face. One of the best things she had gotten from Grandma was inheriting her joy of cooking. It was one of Katherine's passions in life and had become so much a part of her inner soul and who she was.

After she and Jason returned from the market on Wednesday, she set herself to preparing whatever she could ahead of time to make tomorrow easier. She was preparing all her grandmother's favorites: turkey with sage stuffing, mashed potatoes, collards, buttered carrots with dill, corn pudding, buttermilk biscuits, and, of course, her towering chocolate cake and apple pie.

Her Grandpa entered the kitchen and said, "If I didn't know better, I'd expect Elizabeth to be standing in here. Thank you for doing all of this, my sweet Katie. It's bittersweet."

Katherine walked over to her grandpa and encircled him in a warm embrace. "I love you so much, Grandpa. There is nothing I wouldn't do for you. You've been more like a father to me than a grandfather, and I'm so grateful."

On Thanksgiving morning, she was already in the kitchen when Melanie arrived. "I'm here to help, Kat. Just tell me what to do."

"Everything's under control in here, but we could start setting the table."

The dining room was just off the kitchen, beyond an arched entryway. The large mahogany dining table had been there for as long as the girls could remember. Elizabeth had sewn long drapes for the large window overlooking some of her gardens, and she had covered the seat cushions in the same fabric. The sideboard table was along one wall and was the perfect place for the desserts. There was a gorgeous oriental rug under the table that pulled the colors in the room together. Katherine gazed at the rug, remembering that as a child, her grandma would give her a tiny brush and let her brush the rug's bangs, as little Katherine referred to them. They pulled out the tablecloth, fine China, silver, and crystal that was always used for special occasions. Katherine had picked up a flower arrangement from Dottie's florist.

"Your mom and dad should be here soon, so we can bring the food in and set it on the table as soon as they get here."

"Oh, I am so looking forward to spending the afternoon with my mother," Melanie said sarcastically.

"I'm sure she will be on her best behavior today, Mel. She never shows her bad side in front of Grandpa, but he still knows how she is, anyway. She's bringing freshly brewed tea and the wine, at least."

"I promise to play nice in the sandbox as long as she does, Kat."

Just then, they heard, "Yoo-hoo, where is everybody?"

"Oh marvelous, Cruella has arrived," Melanie said, rolling her eyes

Katherine giggled, pointing her finger at Melanie.

Regina entered the dining room and put her hand on her chest. "Oh, Katherine, this looks lovely. How on earth did you manage to do all of this on your own?"

"Hi, Aunt Regina. Thanks. Melanie and I have been at work all day."

"Now, Katherine, I'm sure Melanie had nothing to do with any of this. Why, she can't even boil a potato without burning it. She does not have the cooking and domestic skills that you do."

"Well, of course I do, Mother. I got all my skills from you as I was growing up, remember?"

Regina glared at Melanie. Attempting to break the tension, Katherine said, "I think we need to get the food on the table and call in the guys to come and eat before everything gets cold."

Their dinner went well, with less tension in the air. At one point, Regina said, "Katherine, this gravy is the best I have ever had."

"I couldn't agree with you more, Aunt Regina. Melanie made it."

Melanie choked on the water she had just taken a sip of. "Excuse me, everybody. I swallowed wrong."

Offering no kind of compliment to her daughter, Regina said, "Well, Melanie, you need to give me your recipe."

At that point, Katherine rose from the table and went into the kitchen to get the pitcher of tea to refill everyone's glasses. Melanie followed her.

She grabbed Katherine's arm and whispered, "Why did you tell my mother that I made the gravy? Now she wants my frigging recipe."

"Because I'm fed up with your mother never giving you credit for anything."

"That's probably because I don't deserve it."

"Yes, you do– and by the way, I'll email you the recipe."

After dinner, they went into the parlor to have their dessert and coffee while sitting in front of the fire Jason had made. After a while, Melanie stood, saying she was tired and wanted to go lie down. "You know us expectant mommies need our rest." She smiled at everyone except her mother. She hugged

Katherine, thanking her for helping to make the day so special for all of them, and then hugged her grandpa, telling him how much she loved him.

She went up to the room that had been hers when she stayed over as a little girl growing up. She curled up on the bed, covering herself with the quilt her grandmother had made for her, hugging a pillow. Instead of sleeping, she cried. *Why doesn't my mother love me? I've never even heard her say the words to me. I wish she and I could be close, especially now that I'm having a baby. I won't allow myself to be like her. I'm going to be a good mother. My baby will know he or she is loved and treasured.* She eventually drifted off to sleep, dreaming sweet dreams of her life with Chris and their baby.

Chapter Eleven

Christmas was approaching before she knew it. Katherine went down to her grandpa's a week early so she could make the house look festive. She thought it might be nice to make the holiday a little different from usual. Melanie had agreed with her it might be better for Grandpa. Together, they had an open house on Christmas Eve, inviting close family friends and a few church members. As the girls predicted, their grandpa seemed to thoroughly enjoy the evening. Katherine had noticed, though, that one woman from the church seemed to have a little too much interest in Ben, barely leaving his side and acting in a slightly flirtatious manner. She dismissed it as being of no importance.

Christmas morning, the girls thought it might be a delightful change to have an abundant brunch instead of the more formal Christmas dinner they had had in the past. Ben was quiet, and his unspoken feelings showed on his face.

After brunch, everyone went into the parlor and opened gifts around the tree with Christmas music playing on the stereo. Katherine and Jason had given gifts for the baby to Melanie and Chris. Melanie squealed with joy when she opened the beautifully wrapped package. They had given Grandpa a gorgeous pocket watch with a picture of Elizabeth on one side of the inside. They engraved it on the opposite side of the picture with the words *Always in your heart.* He was silent when he opened it and held it in the palm of his hands as if it were an egg that might break. When he finally looked up, there were tears in his sunken eyes as he looked over at Katherine and Jason.

"My precious Katie and Jason, you do not know how much this means to me. Now, I will always have my Elizabeth with me." Katherine went over and wrapped her arms around him where he sat.

"I'm so happy you like it, Grandpa. We love you so much."

Despite Regina's lack of joyous behavior, they all had a wonderful time. It was always like this. She couldn't allow herself to let go and join in during a celebration of any kind.

Jason had to go back to work the day after Christmas, but Katherine stayed so she and Melanie could talk about plans for her nursery. He was returning in a week so he and Katherine could spend New Year with Chris and Melanie and help them work on the nursery. To their amazement, Dan and Regina had invited Ben to go to the club with them on New Year's Eve.

None of them wanted to go to a loud party, so they decided instead to spend the evening at Chris and Melanie's house and make a nice dinner together. The guys put a prime rib on a slow roast on the gas grill out on the patio while the girls put together a green salad and mashed potatoes. Katherine made a strawberry chiffon cake for dessert.

While the meat was slowly cooking, they gathered in the center of the patio, around the fire pit, surrounded by large, comfortable chairs. Jason and Chris opened a beer, and Katherine and Melanie wrapped up in warm, Cuddl Duds blankets. Katherine had wine, and Melanie had hot chocolate. They talked well into the night until Melanie stood, announcing that if she didn't get to bed soon, she might turn into a pumpkin. Chris said teasingly, "Hmmm, I can see a small resemblance." Melanie grinned, rubbing her rather enormous belly as the others laughed. It didn't bother her one bit. First, she knew Chris was lovingly teasing, and second, she loved the way she looked, and she loved knowing that in the not too far future, their baby would arrive. After they all exchanged New Year's hugs and kisses, Chris and Melanie headed back inside.

Jason and Katherine embraced, and she said, "I am really looking forward to starting our family."

"Then what are we doing wasting our time out here? I say let's go work on it." And he scooped her up in his arms as if she weighed merely a feather and headed in the house. Katherine giggled the entire time.

They were able to stay two more days before they needed to head back. Jason helped Chris assemble the crib and other small pieces of furniture for the room. Katherine, using her grandmother's sewing machine, made delicate curtains for the window and a full bed skirt under the crib. They had ultimately decided to wait to find out the child's gender, so they had picked colors that would work for either a boy or a girl in soft hues of yellow, mint green, and white. Using water-based safe paint, Melanie was finishing up the final touches on the large mural she was painting on the wall across from the crib. It was of a large, curved rainbow with white puffy clouds and tiny birds and grass along the baseboard, with flowers and colorful mushrooms like those in children's picture books.

After cleaning up, they all stood back and admired the room they had worked so hard to create.

"I think the four of us make a pretty good team," Jason said. Chris put his arm around his shoulder, shaking his hand at the same time.

"We sure do, brother. Couldn't have done it without you. Thank you to both of you."

Somehow, none of them had noticed that Melanie was sitting in the rocker just a few feet from them. She was incredibly quiet. Melanie was rarely quiet. Chris went and kneeled in front of her. Seeing the tears slowly rolling down her cheeks, he said, "Sweetheart, what's wrong? If there's anything you don't like, don't worry. I'll work day and night to change it."

"I'm just so overwhelmed with happiness, Chris. There are just no words to describe how I feel."

"I feel the same way, babe. We have so much to look forward to."

Watching them made Katherine's eyes fill up with tears. She was so truly happy for them and excited about the baby. Jason put his arm around her and pulled her toward him. This was going to be a special time for all of them. He hoped Katherine could conceive before he left for his next deployment.

. . .

The time arrived for Jason and Katherine to head back home. They exchanged last hugs at their cars, promising to get together again before Jason left on the deployment.

Their schedules had prevented them from getting together, so Chris and Melanie drove up to spend a couple of days to have some time with Jason before he left. The day of his deployment was very busy. He had a lot of work to do to make sure his Marines were ready and had all their gear together. Once completed, he joined Katherine, Melanie, and Chris at the picnic area where all the other families were waiting to say goodbye. As was always the case in the Marines, the phrase *hurry up and wait* applied. They ended up having two hours more time together, which was not a bad thing. There were tables set up throughout the area with water and snacks for the hundreds waiting. When the time arrived for them to leave, there was not much time to say their last goodbyes. Jason gave Melanie a big hug and shook Chris's hand, and then embraced Katherine in a hug, followed by a long kiss.

"I'll meet you right back here, beautiful, I promise. Hopefully, our marathon from last night will pay off, and you'll be pregnant when I return."

"I hope so, but I'll be fat and not at all sexy."

"Not possible. You'd be sexy and beautiful to me even if you weighed 300 lbs."

"I love you so much, Jason. My life would be nothing without you."

"We'll always have each other, Kat."

With tears in her eyes, Katherine watched him go. Deployments were a part of their life but never got easier. Chris and Melanie stayed until the following morning before leaving.

. . .

Katherine did not get pregnant as she had hoped. Mother nature had reared her ugly head two weeks after Jason left. She was a little depressed for about a week because she had wanted this so badly. She continued to stay busy tutoring Marines that were still on the base, and she got involved in as many volunteer opportunities as possible. She was also checking schools in the area and online programs to earn her Ph.D. She might as well try to get it behind her as soon as possible since she and Jason had decided to start a family earlier in their marriage than they had originally planned.

She drove down the middle of March for the baby shower she was throwing for Melanie. She had had it at Melanie's house so as not to disturb their grandpa, as well as not having to pack up the gifts to haul back to Melanie's after the shower. It was a ton of fun, and Melanie's friends and co-workers were very generous. Even Regina was there and had given her many things on her gift registry, as well as a three-in-one stroller that was extremely expensive. She had been rather quiet during the shower, but Melanie seemed not to notice. Katherine thought it just meant a lot to her that she was there at all.

Katherine stayed five extra days to help Melanie get the baby clothes washed and put away, and to organize all the other gifts she had received. When she was leaving and saying good-bye, she said, "Have Chris call me if you go into labor."

"I certainly hope it's soon, Kat, I feel like a whale and can hardly move. Thank you for everything you always do for me. I love and appreciate you more than you know."

. . .

Just three weeks later, Katherine's phone rang at four in the morning. Chris, on the other end, sounded hysterical, saying Melanie's water had broken, and she was in labor. He sounded so cute and pitiful all at the same time. Katherine felt a little laugh coming, but held it in. She assured him that everything would be fine and that she would be on the road within the hour.

She packed in record time, taking extra clothes with her so she could stay as long as they needed her. She was on the road by five. At around six, she dialed Regina's number. She answered, sounding rather somnolent.

"Good morning, Aunt Regina."

"Katherine, why on earth are you calling at this hour? The sun isn't even up yet."

"Hasn't Chris called you? Melanie's in labor."

"Well, yes, he did a couple of hours ago. I told him I'd be over later; after all, I have my bridge club today and babies take hours to be born, anyway. I'd just as soon not sit around the hospital and wait. I'll see you later on, sweetie."

Katherine could not believe what she was hearing. Regina had not been a nurturing mother. That common knowledge, but to not go to her daughter's side when she was in labor, was just plain callous. Apparently, she was even more self-absorbed than Katherine had realized. She knew it hurt Melanie deeply that her mother was the way she was. She needed help to deal with that, especially now that she was going to have a child of her own.

She arrived at the hospital and was directed to labor and

delivery. She discovered Chris pacing outside the door to Melanie's room, dressed in scrubs.

She quickly made her way down the corridor to him.

"How is she?"

"The doctor's in with her now but he says everything is moving along nicely and does not expect any complications."

"Then why are you pacing up and down the hall?"

"Just feeling anxious, I guess."

"Well, you might want to slow down there, cowboy, before you wear out part of the floor."

Her attempt to get him laughing paid off. He seemed to relax a little and just smiled. Just then, the doctor came out.

"You can go back in now, Mr. Sandston. It won't be much longer. I just need to check on something, but I'll be right back."

Katherine went to one side of Melanie's bed, and Chris went to the other. She looked tired but serene.

"Have either of you seen my mama?"

"I'm sure she'll be here soon. She's probably just caught up in traffic," Katherine lied, glancing at Chris.

Another contraction came, and Melanie worked through it with bravery. Chris was right with her, coaching her on. The doctor reentered the room, followed by the nurse. He positioned himself at the foot of Melanie's bed. The nurse helped Melanie position herself into the stirrups.

"On the next contraction, I need you to push hard, Melanie," the doctor instructed.

It only took two more pushes for the doctor to deliver the baby. Melanie heard the baby cry and tears were rolling down her face.

"Congratulations, you have a baby girl."

. . .

The doctor placed the baby on Melanie's chest and when it was time to do so, Chris cut the cord. Shortly thereafter, the nurse took her briefly to clean her up, wrap her up in a blanket, and brought her back to Melanie. Chris wrapped one arm around Melanie's neck and the other around her and their little girl. They were both crying tears of pure joy. Katherine had backed away to give them their time but grabbed her cell phone out of her pocket and started snapping pictures to capture the moment for them. It was indeed a beautiful sight.

After a few minutes, Melanie looked over at Katherine saying, "Come meet your goddaughter."

As Katherine made her way to the side of the bed, she already had tears streaming down her face. She accepted the baby from Melanie, saying at the same time, "I'm her godmother?"

"Well, of course. Who else would we trust to take care of our daughter if anything were to happen to us?"

Katherine just gazed down at the baby, loving the feel of holding her. "Hello, little one. I'm going to love you forever. Have you guys decided on a name for this bundle of joy yet?"

Melanie looked at Chris and he nodded. "Sophia Rose. Her middle name, Rose, is in honor of Grandma because of her love for roses."

"Oh, that is so beautiful. It would have meant the world to Grandma and oh, how she would have loved this little girl."

"Could one of you see if my mama and daddy are here?"

Katherine glanced at Chris with a look of worry in her eyes that Melanie didn't see. He quickly said, "I'll go find them, sweetheart."

. . .

When he stepped out into the hallway, he immediately saw Dan. "How's my little girl?"

"She could not be better and is holding our little girl."

Dan patted him on the back, saying, "Congratulations, son. When can I see them both?"

"You're good to come in now. The doctor's finished. Where's Regina? Melanie has been asking for her."

Dan looked at him with a despondent look on his face. "You know Regina. It's all about her and what she wants. I love my wife, but she disappoints me at times. I sent her a text message letting her know I was heading to the hospital. She sent me back a message stating she would come after her bridge club. She didn't even ask me to let her know what I found out when I got to the hospital. Her way of thinking is beyond my realm of comprehension."

"I don't know what to tell Melanie, Dan. She's going to be so disappointed. I don't want to say anything to upset her."

"Let's just tell her that her mother is on her way and leave it at that."

Chris agreed it was probably the best way to handle it. He led Dan into Melanie's room, and her face lit up like a light when she saw him.

"Oh, Daddy, you're here. Come meet your granddaughter."

He went to Melanie and wrapped his arms around her. "Hi, kitten. Are you doing okay?"

"I feel fabulous, Daddy. I'm just a little tired. Here, take your granddaughter. She's dying to meet you. Is Mama here too?"

"Not yet, but she'll be here soon." To change the subject, he looked down at the baby he was holding, then back at Melanie. "I'm so proud of you, sweetheart. She's beautiful, just like you."

"Thank you, Daddy. Chris's parents are flying in

tomorrow from Texas. We might get to go home tomorrow night; if not, it should be the next morning. I can't wait to take her home."

Regina finally showed up at 3:00 that afternoon. Dan was still there. Melanie had been sleeping when she arrived, so thankfully was not aware of how long it had taken her Mother to get there.

"Mama," she exclaimed when she woke up, "you're here."

"Well, of course I am, darling. Where else would I be on a day like this?"

"You can go pick up your new granddaughter. She wants to meet her Grandma."

"Oh, no. I don't want to be called Grandma. Sounds too much like an old, gray-haired woman. I'd prefer Nana."

She went and picked her up out of the bassinet. She didn't say any of the sweet things her daddy had said. Only that she was so precious. Melanie could tell right away that she was going to be the same kind of grandmother as she had been as a mother. Again, Melanie thought to herself, *what's it going to take?*

Chapter Twelve

Chris's parents, Robert and Suzanne, arrived at 11:00 the following morning and were at the hospital by 12:30. Chris had called them after the baby was born to tell them all the details, including the baby's name.

They bustled into Melanie's room full of excitement, going immediately to the bed and embracing her in warm hugs and light kisses on her cheek.

His mother then embraced Chris like she didn't want to let go, saying, "Oh, how I've missed you. I'm so happy for you and Melanie."

His father hugged him too, and then backed away just slightly, leaving one hand on his shoulder. "I love you, son. Congratulations. Oh, and by the way, I stopped in the gift shop downstairs and picked up some of these for you." He handed Chris cigars that said, "It's a girl!"

Chris laughed. "Thanks, Dad. We'll have to light one of these up later when we get back to the house."

His mother had already gone to the bassinet and picked up the baby. She was sitting in the chair next to Melanie's bed with tears of joy streaming down her face. "This is the most beautiful baby girl I have ever seen. Hello there, little miss Sophia. Then she said to Melanie, "I think we may just need to move closer to you so we can be there as she grows up. We'd be fabulous babysitters, and your kids could go out whenever the mood hits you."

Melanie was laughing now. "Be careful what you offer, Suzanne; we might just take you up on it."

"I'm being as serious as a preacher. A child needs to spend time with their grandma and grandpa. Oh, is it alright if she calls us that? Your parents should have the first pick on what they want to be called."

"It's perfectly fine; in fact, it's what I'd prefer. My Mother wants to be called Nana and my dad is going to be called Papa, so she doesn't get confused with her great-grandfather being called Grandpa."

"That sounds like a wonderful decision. Now, precious, when do you and this little angel get to go home?"

"The doctor said we could go home later tonight. He said both Sophia and I are doing just fine, so he doesn't see any reason to keep us."

They left the hospital at six o'clock that night. Robert and Suzanne had been there all day and Dan came back again later in the day, bringing along his dad. Regina said she didn't go because she felt there would be too many people there, but she had never really liked Suzanne. She felt she was beneath her. Suzanne was very down-to-earth and sincere. She didn't worry about having designer clothes, or the finest house or car. What she treasured in life was the love of family and often staid that if you had that, you had all the wealth in the world. Regina thought her to be too simple-minded and lacking class.

As soon as Katherine found out Melanie would be going home, she left the hospital so she could get everything ready. She stopped by the market to pick up something to make for dinner. She prepared a large chicken roaster, mashed potatoes, green beans, apple sauce, buttermilk biscuits, and peach cobbler for dessert. It was somewhat challenging to cook in Melanie's kitchen. While Melanie cooked some, she didn't make the creations Katherine did, so the cookware was limited. But she made it work.

After putting the roast in the oven, she went to check upstairs. She cleaned the guest bathroom and changed the sheets in the guest room for Robert and Suzanne. She tidied up Chris and Melanie's room and made sure their bathroom was clean, as well. Lastly, she went into the nursery. Everything had been ready for weeks, so there was really nothing she needed to do. She loved this room. It already smelled like a baby since they had washed everything in Dreft before putting it away. She picked up the white teddy bear out of the crib and holding it, went over, and sat down in the rocker. She felt so happy and disconsolate all at the same time. While she was over the moon, happy for Melanie and Chris, she had a slight ache in her heart over not having conceived before Jason left. Even though they had only just decided a few months ago to step up their plans of starting a family sooner than originally planned, she had become more and more anxious about it. She knew they would have several children. That had always been a desire for them both.

She decided to get off her pity pot and go down to finish getting everything ready. She searched through cabinets and drawers until she finally found a tablecloth that needed ironing. Once she had taken care of that, she set one of the flower arrangements that had arrived for Melanie in the center of the table and found some white candles. She set enough place settings for seven. That would cover herself, Ben, Dan, Chris's parents, Chris, and Melanie. Regina said she would, of course, not be joining them. She had told Katherine that she had a terrible migraine. Katherine knew it was a lie.

Just as she was finishing the food preparation, she heard

the cars pulling up. Melanie was the first in the door, followed by Chris, carrying Sophia's baby carrier. What a sweet sight it was. Melanie was all aglow. One could never have imagined she had just had a baby less than forty-eight hours ago. Katherine threw her arms around her, giving her a big hug.

"Welcome home, Mama. You look wonderful."

"I love you, Kat." The house smelled wonderful from all the cooking, causing Melanie to look toward the kitchen. She could see the table and how lovely it looked. "Oh, how beautiful. Thank you for this. What a wonderful welcome home. Where's Mama?"

Katherine did not quite know what to say and had to think quickly. "I think I heard she had a headache and would not be coming, but I'm sure she'll be over when she's feeling better tomorrow." The expression on Melanie's face looked dismayed but quickly changed. There was no way she was going to let her Mother ruin this time for her. If she came, she came. If she didn't, she didn't. Melanie told herself she would accept whatever she would get from her Mother and accept what she didn't. She convinced herself to have low expectations.

Dinner had been exceptional, as were all the meals Katherine prepared. That she paid so much attention to the minor details and cooked from the heart flourished in every meal she made. As with prior occasions, Katherine thoroughly enjoyed Robert and Suzanne. It was also quite clear that they adored Chris and loved Melanie as if she were their daughter. Suzanne insisted on cleaning up after dinner.

"It's the least I can do to help after you prepared this scrumptious meal, Katherine. You take yourself on out of here and go spend some time with Melanie and that precious baby."

Katherine went over and gave her a brief hug and thanked her. She followed Melanie out of the room and into the family room, where she had been saying goodnight to everyone. Katherine told Chris to stay and enjoy everyone's company and that she would help Melanie get ready and into bed.

"I don't know whatever I did to deserve you and all that you do for me, Kat."

"You were born; that's what you did," she said, laughing. "You know we've always been like sisters. You'd do the same for me if I were ever in need of anything."

"You know I would, but I could never do it as well as you." She was already curled up in the bed and fighting the sleep that was overcoming her. Katherine kissed her forehead. "Sweet dreams, I love you."

She had thought Melanie was already asleep but overheard her saying as she was leaving the room, "Love you more."

Robert and Suzanne stayed for several days but had to fly out on Sunday. Suzanne had tears in her eyes when she had to say goodbye to Melanie. "If I had chosen a wife for my son, I would have chosen you. You are a wonderful and loving person. Now, make sure you give that baby over there a kiss every day and tell her it's from her grandma. Don't you dare forget to call on us if you need anything at all!" She was stalling, saying anything and everything to keep from having to walk away, but finally, she laid her hand along Melanie's cheek, gently stroked it, and then turned toward the car Chris already had waiting to drive them to the airport.

Katherine stayed for another week, making the short drive back and forth from her grandpa's. Melanie had wanted her to stay at their house, but Katherine had felt that they needed time alone to enjoy being just the three of them, and she wanted to spend some quality time with her grandpa.

During the days when she was with Melanie, she waited on her hand and foot, even with Melanie protesting the entire time.

"Kat, you don't need to do this. I'm completely capable."

"Of course you are, but I want to do whatever I can for you. Plus, you need to get plenty of rest. Those middle-of-the-night feedings are going to last for a while."

She finally relented. She knew she would not win a battle with Katherine.

One afternoon, Melanie was sitting on the couch, her head resting on the back with her legs stretched out. She had a distressed expression on her face. Sophia was asleep, curled up on her chest, having just finished nursing. Katherine had been sitting in the chair across from her, using the ottoman to fold baby clothes that had just come out of the dryer. Studying her, she knew what was going through Melanie's mind. Regina had only stopped over twice and never stayed long. Melanie always seemed despondent after her visits. Katherine knew she had to try to help the two women. They mixed like oil and vinegar and sparred often. No time like the present to take the plunge, she decided.

"You know.... You're going to have to make the first move with her."

"What do you have, telepathy or something? How did you know what I was thinking about?"

"Oh, please, Mel. You and I have been attached at the hip our entire lives. I always know what you're thinking and feeling, for that matter."

"I don't know where to begin, Kat. When I was growing up, the way my mother was bothered me, and I was always envious of my friends who had nurturing moms, but this feels different. I, for whatever reason, need to be able to connect with my mother now that I'm a mother."

"Take it slow. She will not change her ways, at least not at first, but you can change how you react to her. I think it would be helpful if you let her know when she says things that hurt you or put you down. Your entire life, you had low expectations of her, but that's changed now, and I can understand that. Try talking to her about something normal that might interest her, or maybe you could ask her about her childhood with your grandmother. Try to get her to talk about it and put yourself in her shoes."

"I guess I could try that. We've rarely ever talked about anything important. She always made sure I had everything I needed growing up, but I never felt like I had her heart or that she loved me deeply. She told me I was an 'accident' at one point and that she had not wanted children. The love I have for Sophia is the most intense love I've ever had. Even different from the love I have for Chris. How could she not feel that?"

"I've heard that from people before once they have children. It's almost obsessive. There's one other thing, Mel, and this is a big one. You need to forgive her. More for yourself than for her. It's not that you'd be saying all the things she's done or said are OK, but it may help you move forward in the here and now and leave the past where it belongs: in the past."

"How'd you get so smart, Kat? I've always been so annoyed with her that I never even contemplated trying any of what you've suggested. I feel better already. Next time I see her, I'm going to give it a go. What's the worst that could happen?"

Chapter Thirteen

Melanie went to bed that night, full of high hopes. She knew she couldn't set her expectations too high after all; she and her mother had a lot of weeds to sift through before getting to a place where they both could be happy. She also could accept the fact that she had not done the relationship any good by the way she reacted to her mother. She allowed her mother to push her buttons and came out fighting like a cat. A softer approach would surely work better. Kill her with kindness, as the saying goes. She would call her in the morning to set the wheels in motion.

* * *

"Good morning, Mama. What are you doing today?"

Regina was silent at first, probably from the shock of Melanie calling her and the bubbliness in her voice, "Well, good morning to you too, Melanie. My, you sound so good today. I'm having lunch with my friend Gladys. Why do you ask?" It caused her to be suspicious. Melanie never appeared to care what she was doing.

"No special reason. I was hoping maybe you could stop by, or we could come over and see you. I haven't seen you in days."

"Who's we?" Again, feeling uncomfortable

"Me and Sophia, of course. Who else would I be referring to?" *Careful, Melanie, you're using that tone with her again.* "I'm sorry, Mama, I meant to say only the baby and me. Chris is at work, and Katherine's spending the day with Grandpa. She's going to be heading back up to Camp Lejeune tomorrow."

"Oh, I see. Well, I could leave a little early and come by on my way to lunch. Would that work?"

"Perfectly. I'll see you when you get here. Love you, Mama."

"Okay."

Melanie ended the call, frowning. *Okay.... Really???*

Regina arrived at Melanie's at 11:00. She let herself in and found Melanie in the kitchen making a bottle for the baby.

"I'm here. I thought you said you were going to breastfeed. Why the bottle?"

"Oh, hi, Mama. I'm trying to get her used to so Chris can feed her too. I use a breast pump, so she always gets breast milk."

"My goodness, how things have changed. We didn't have those sorts of fancy gadgets when you were a baby and even if they did, I wouldn't have used them."

"Why don't you go sit in a comfortable chair? You can feed her if you'd like."

"Oh, I don't think I should. This is a linen blouse I have on, and I wouldn't want to get it messed up or, heaven forbid, thrown up on."

Take a deep breath, Melanie. Don't strike out at her. They did not build Rome in a day. "I can understand that, Mama.

90

Here, I have this large baby blanket. We can spread it in front of you just in case you like."

Almost bashfully, Regina replied, "Well, yes, that should work out just fine." She wasn't accustomed to seeing Melanie react this way to her, and as pleasant as it was, it was also a little unsettling.

Melanie sat on the sofa and watched as her mother fed Sophia. She had such a warm expression on her face as she gazed down at her grandchild. She looked so peaceful. It was a moment in time she wanted to freeze. She reached for her cell phone and took several pictures, capturing the moment.

"She has your hands, Melanie. She's so beautiful."

"Thank you, Mama. Mama, what was your childhood like? You've never really talked about it much– or about Papa Ed, who I never even met."

Her Mother's expression suddenly took on a disquieted look, as if a cloud had just covered up the sun.

"I'd prefer not to talk about my childhood, Melanie. That was a long time ago. I'd especially prefer not to talk about Papa Ed. The world became a better place once that man was dead."

Everything about her mother had suddenly changed. Her peaceful mood and calm from before were gone. Her countenance had become hard and angry. Melanie was so regretful for broaching the subject with her. She had only been attempting to dig deeper into her mother's past to uncover what may have made her the way she was. Her mother always seemed to keep people at arms-length. As far as Melanie knew, she had never had any devoted relationships with other women.

What in the world happened in my mother's past? It has to have been something awful, considering the transformation that occurred when I brought it up. I need to know what it was, but I will not ask her again. I can't remember ever having met my grandmother, although I think I remember my mother telling me she took me to see her when I was a baby. She and my mother don't have a relationship, so asking her is out of the question. There's something out there that I need to find out. I need to find someone else who can provide me with the answers.

* * *

Katherine left the next morning. She had stayed long enough, and Melanie was doing great. She didn't really need her anymore. When she returned home, she planned to check into Ph.D. programs, possibly online again. When she got pregnant, it would make life easier, especially if she had any issues or morning sickness. Having been tutoring the Marines the past couple of years had reignited her desire to teach at the college level. She called Melanie when she got home. They had not had time to talk, before she left, about how things went with her mother's visit. She gave Katherine a rundown, but what she talked about most was how her mother reacted when she asked about her childhood.

"I'm telling you, Kat, it was as if something overtook her. Everything about her changed as quickly as flipping a light switch. One minute she was holding Sophia, looking peaceful, and the next, she transformed into looking like a wounded animal. She wouldn't tell me anything, but I'm going to find a way to discover why."

"Let me know when you find out, okay?"

"I will. Sophia's awake. Duty calls. I'll call you soon. Love you."

"Love you more."

When Katherine hung up the phone, she had a feeling of regret. She was not normally a judgmental person, but she had always had some feelings of aversion to her aunt. She was not a good mother on so many levels. Actually, she should have never been a mother. Whatever this was could very well explain a few things. She was as eager as Melanie was for the answer.

Chapter Fourteen

Melanie had difficulty sleeping when she went to bed that night. She kept thinking of her mother, with all sorts of scenarios running through her head of things that may have made her mother the way she is. Before drifting off to sleep, she decided she would call her father in the morning. If anyone knew anything, he would.

She called him the next morning but got his voicemail. She left him a message telling him there was something she needed to talk to him about but asked him not to communicate that to her mother.

He called her back later that morning and agreed to stop by after work that afternoon.

When Melanie opened the door for him, she was holding Sophia.

His smile lit up the room when he saw her. He reached to take her from Melanie. "How's my precious granddaughter?" He cuddled her closely, making goo-goo noises at her and kissing her all over. It warmed Melanie's heart. She asked him to join her in the family room so they could talk. She gathered Sophia from his arms and placed her in the cradle by the fireplace. He considered Melanie's serious expression as he lowered himself into a chair across from her.

"What has you so troubled, kitten? Is everything okay with you and Chris? Are you ill?"

"We're fine, and I'm fine. Daddy, what happened to Mama in her childhood? Has she ever shared anything with you? I asked her about it, and she wouldn't even talk about it."

Dan's expression darkened. "Why do you want to know about your mother's childhood all of a sudden?"

"I want to improve my relationship with her. We've always been at odds with each other. I want to change all of that. I feel like if I knew more about her life, I could understand her better."

Dan stood and walked to the window, gazing out. Melanie just stayed where she was watching him, her anxiety growing deeper. Now, even more than ever, she needed to know what had happened to her mother, and her intuition told her that her dad knew something. He spoke without turning around.

"Melanie, what I'm about to tell you is going to be hard for you to hear, but I suppose it's time you knew. She and I have not spoken of it since before you were born."

Then he turned and went back to where he had been sitting. As he sat on the edge of the chair, his head was tilted down toward the rug. His hands were clasped together between his legs, and his elbows were resting on his knees. He slowly raised his head and looked her in the eye as he began to speak.

"Your Mother and I met when we were in high school. She was a beautiful girl with long, brown hair. I became attracted to her as soon as I saw her, but she was a loner. She kept totally to herself, not hanging out with any of the other girls her age, and I never saw her appearing to date any of the boys. It was as if she wanted to be invisible. To my good fortune, we were assigned to be lab partners in biology class. She didn't talk to me unless she had to, and it was always only about the project we were working on. She kept it strictly to our assignment. Eventually, though, I was able to break through the armor that encompassed her, and we became friends. She was not close at first, but then she came to trust me. We spent time together in and out of school. She'd agree to go to the soda shop with me and occasionally to a movie." He smiled before he continued. "I became quite smitten with her but instinctively knew that I couldn't rush her, so I didn't tell her I loved her even though I knew I did.

"I often noticed hideous bruises on her arms and neck, but when I commented on them, she would get embarrassed and quickly pull a sleeve down or do whatever she could to cover it. She told me she had a disorder that caused bruising. I didn't believe her but didn't press further."

"It was toward the end of our senior year when I noticed a dramatic change in her. We were walking, holding hands, and heading to the park to hang out one day after school. Your mother loved to go there and feed the ducks near a small pond. We were sitting on the bench under a large tree, shading ourselves from the intense sun rays. She had been so quiet, but I didn't know why, but then she turned to me with tears in her eyes. She looked at me and said, *Daniel, I cannot see you anymore. I'm going away. I can't tell you why, but I have to. I don't know when or even if I'll ever return.* I turned toward her and placed my hands on each of her arms, begging her to tell me why. I confessed to her I loved her and could not let her go. She began to cry hysterically. Her entire body was shaking, and she appeared to be losing control. It was at that point that she confessed the truth to me.

"When your Mother was very young, your grandmother and grandfather were divorced."

"You mean Grandpa Ed was not my real grandfather?"

Dan's face assumed a somber look. "No, Melanie, he was

not. Your grandmother married him when your mother was four. He was her stepfather. From what your mother told me, she never saw her father again but does not know why. Her stepfather was a hard, cruel man. If he told her to do something and she didn't do it right, he would beat her. He didn't leave marks that could be seen at first, but they were there. He threw her down a flight of stairs once when she was twelve because she had not remembered to turn off the bathroom light, causing her to break her leg. He and her mother took her to the hospital, telling them she had fallen off her bike. He had eyeballed your mother the entire time, warning her with the unspoken consequence that would happen should she tell the truth."

"Why didn't Gran Ann do anything about it or take my mother and just leave?"

"She was and still is a very weak woman. He was a formidable man with a lot of power in the community and threatened to kill her if she ever said or did anything against him."

"So, is being abused as a child the reason Mama's the way she is?"

"No, Kitten. There's more. Much more.

"As I was saying, your mother was physically and emotionally abused when she was young, but it got worse. When she was fourteen, he began to sexually abuse her. When she would go to bed at night, she would pray in the dark that he would not enter her room. If she locked her door to prevent him from accessing her room, the sexual abuse would be more brutal. She felt so dirty and ashamed as if it was her fault.

"That day in the park, when she confessed everything to me, she seemed so damaged and alone. Through her sobs, she told me the rest. She had discovered just that morning she was pregnant with his child. She went to your grandmother, who exploded. She blamed your mother and said she was nothing more than a little tramp who had seduced him. She told your mother she needed to leave. Having a stepdaughter become pregnant out of wedlock would be a disgrace to Edward, and the consequences he would bring down on them would be horrific. He would have let nothing, or anyone, affect his standing in the community."

"She was incredibly alone, and there was no way I would have allowed her to leave on her own. We were both eighteen, so we did not need our parents' permission. We eloped, going to a justice of the peace where we lived and were married. I told her I would love and take care of her and her baby for the rest of our lives."

Melanie had tears in her eyes, not for herself, but from hearing of the pain, her mother had endured.

"So, Daddy, are you telling me I was the baby she was pregnant with?"

He hesitated before answering, not wanting to say the words. "Yes, Kitten, you were."

"So, you're not my real father?"

"No, Kitten, I'm not, but I've loved you since before you were born and always thought of you as my child. I would not have felt any differently even if I had been the one that had impregnated your mother."

She was stunned at being told this information, but it didn't change the love she felt for her dad. He had always been loving and kind. He made her feel cherished. Even knowing what she knew now, she would never think of him any differently.

"That would explain why I have blue eyes unlike brown like you and Mama. I'm curious to see what he looked like and whether I have any of his features. I hope I don't. I hate that sick man and what he did to Mama. I guess that's the reason Mama and I have never been close. Does looking at me serve as a constant reminder of what happened to her?"

"It might have, at first. I'm sorry to say she didn't want to have anything to do with you once you were born. She was so full of bitterness. I remember her saying, 'Thank God that thing is finally out of me.' She wouldn't hold you or help to take care of you. Because I was in the insurance business, I could work from home and take care of you. When I needed to go out on appointments, I would get a babysitter. Then one afternoon, when you were about two months old, I discovered your mother standing beside your crib, watching you sleep. She was reaching down and rubbing your back. You stirred, and she reached down, picked you up, and went to sit in the rocker that was in your nursery. I watched her as she sat rocking you. She had such a serene, softened look on her face. It was at that moment I knew she had let go of the past and could love you. There was a powerful ambiance in that room. It felt as though I could reach out and touch it. I went in and knelt by her side, saying nothing but just laying my hand on her leg. She didn't look up from gazing at you but said, we won't be needing a babysitter anymore, Daniel. I will take care of our baby. From that moment on, your mother did everything that any mother would do for her child."

Melanie was openly crying at this point. She had no issue in finding out that her biological father was not her dad, but her heart ached for her mother and the cruelty she had endured as a child.

Through her tears, she said. "Oh, Daddy, if Mama was here right now, I'd rush up and hold her in my arms. Thank you for telling me all of this. It helps me understand Mama better and why she always keeps everyone in her life at arms-length. We may never have the kind of relationships like other mothers and daughters, but I'll be able to handle that better now without always feeling so angry with her."

Daniel then stood and walked over to Melanie, who had stood up as well. He wrapped his arms around her, giving her a big bear hug. "I love you so much, my precious Melanie. You'll always be my baby."

"I know that, Daddy. What you told me today won't change a thing between us. You'll always be my daddy. I love you too."

He walked over to bend over and give sleeping Sophia a kiss on her forehead. "This little one is beautiful, just like her mama. You're going to be a wonderful mother, Melanie."

He kissed her on the cheek before walking out the door and getting into his car.

After he left, Melanie sat in a chair, watching her daughter sleep, thinking about the conversation she and her dad had. He had been right; it was hard to hear about all the things that had happened to her mother during her childhood. She loved her mother and now she could love her even more and accept the way she was without animosity toward her. Things were going to be better. She felt at peace, finally having a better understanding. If she could give her mother wonderful memories to replace those in her past, she would try. She wanted her mother to heal from the scars of her past that were still so vividly there. Melanie knew Katherine was right. It was going to be up to her to change things between her and her mother, but she knew she was up to the challenge.

Chapter Fifteen

Katherine tried to call Melanie several times over the past week but kept getting her voicemail. She had no way of knowing that Melanie had been avoiding her calls. Melanie needed to come to terms with what she had found out about her mother before telling Katherine, and she was afraid she would ask. She had always talked to her about anything, but this felt different.

Toward the end of the week, she finally answered Katherine's call. If she kept avoiding her, she might get suspicious.

"Good morning Kat."

"I was starting to worry. I've been trying to reach you all week. Is everything okay?"

"Oh, yes, everything is fine. I've just been really busy. Life certainly changes with a baby in the house. I've discovered that what I plan to do with my days does not always happen. Sophia tends to change my plan," she said, chuckling.

"I'm sure she does. I miss her already. Speaking of discovery, have you been able to find out anything concerning your mother's childhood?"

"I talked to Daddy. There isn't much to it. My grandmother was very cold to her when she was a child and very strict. She was not happy most of the time. She and my grand-father divorced when she was very young. She never knew her father. He had left her for another woman and my grand-mother was very bitter. She took it out on my mother. As soon as they graduated from high school, they eloped. That's pretty much the gist of it." She had said everything fast. She only hoped Katherine bought it.

"That explains a lot of things. If your mother was not nurtured growing up and living in a hostile environment, she would not have been able to learn how to be a mother herself. I can see now why your mother does not have a relationship with her mother. Sadly, her father abandoned her as well."

Melanie felt an incredible sigh of relief. She had gone over again and again in her head what she planned to say to Kather-ine. Apparently, it had worked. Katherine dropped the subject. She changed the subject and told Melanie what she had been doing since she had gotten back home and that she had found an online Ph.D. program she was planning to enroll in that fall. They chatted on for a few more minutes before Sophia interrupted the conversation, crying to be fed, causing them to hang up, but promising each other to get together again soon.

After they ended the call, Katherine sat tapping her fingers with an unconvinced expression on her face. Melanie was hiding something, but she had no idea what it could be. She put it out of her mind and finished up the cleaning she had been doing before getting on the phone with Melanie and then headed out. There were several errands she needed to run today.

She turned down her street, heading back home later, and noticed several of her neighbors huddled together in the house's driveway next door to hers. They all seemed to have grave expressions on their faces. She pulled into her driveway, turned the car off, and reached for the bag of groceries and her purse in the passenger seat next to her before getting out of the car. She walked around the back of her car, intending to head over to her neighbors to find out what was going on when she heard a man's voice behind her.

"Mrs. Kelly."

She had been so distracted seeing her neighbors when she drove down the street that she had not noticed the car parked along the curb in front of her house.

She turned to see the chaplain and colonel standing behind her. She immediately dropped everything she had been holding and fell to her knees, screaming, *"No, No, No."* Her blood-curdling screams could be heard all the way down the block. She sounded like a wounded animal. Vivian, the next-door neighbor, ran to her side. She and the two gentlemen gently took hold of Katherine's arms and slowly raised her, helping her into the house.

Holding her face in her hands, moving her body forward and backward, she said through hysterical weeping, "Please, God, don't let this be happening."

The colonel spoke in a very sympathetic tone. "I'm sorry, Mrs. Kelly. Captain Kelly's vehicle hit a roadside IED, killing all four Marines inside. You have my deepest sympathy for your loss."

Katherine sunk into a quiet shock. Suddenly, she couldn't feel anything. It was as if all the spirit in her body was lifted away. She did know how she would live without Jason and didn't want to.

The chaplain was then by her side. "Is there a family member we can call for you? It's important that you not be alone at a time like this."

Her sobbing had halted. She was just staring straight ahead, not looking at any of them. She said almost in a whisper and with no emotion, "My cousin Melanie Sandston. Her number is on my cell phone."

Melanie had just finished feeding Sophia and was putting her down for a nap when she heard her cell phone ringing. She glanced down, seeing that it was Katherine again. She answered, giggling, "Ya miss me already? We just hung up three hours ago."

"Mrs. Sandston?"

"Yes. Who is this, and why are you on my cousin's phone?"

"This is Colonel Bennett from Camp Lejeune. I'm sorry to have to inform you that Captain Kelly has been killed by a roadside IED. The chaplain and I are with Mrs. Kelly at her home, along with one of her neighbors. She asked that we call you on her behalf."

"Oh, my God. This can't be happening! I will be there as soon as I can, but it will take me several hours to get there. Will someone be with Katherine until I arrive?"

"Yes, Ma'am. I will make certain she is not alone while she waits for you to arrive. You have my condolences."

Melanie ended the call, feeling completely stunned, and began to cry. She knew she needed to hurry but felt like she couldn't put one foot in front of the other. She called Chris at work.

Chris answered and couldn't even understand Melanie. She sounded so hysterical. "Mel, slow down. What happened?"

"It's Jason. He's been killed in action. I just got off the phone with the colonel. They've just told Katherine. We have to go to her, Chris, NOW!!!!"

He promised he would head home right away. Melanie started throwing together essentials she knew they might need for the trip up. She couldn't concentrate. She was so upset. Jason had been like a brother to her, and she didn't know how she was going to comfort Katherine. She packed everything she would need for Sophia. By the time Chris got home, everything was ready to put in the car. They were picking Ben up on the way.

They made the trip in record time, with Chris exceeding the speed limit most of the way. The colonel had told Melanie he would contact the visitors check in so that they would have their pass ready to get onto the base. Chris had barely stopped the car in Katherine's driveway when Melanie already had the car door open. She ran from the car and straight into the house. Vivian stood when she saw Melanie come in. There she saw Katherine wrapped up in a blanket on the couch just staring straight ahead, rubbing her locket as though she were looking for strength from her grandma. Melanie went to sit next to Katherine, wrapping her arms around her.

"I'm here Kat. Chris and Grandpa are too. We've come to take you home."

Katherine was just staring into space in front of her and talked in a monotone. "This was supposed to be my home with Jason. He's not coming back. Did they tell you that? Do you think they could be mistaken? Maybe he was not even in the vehicle and is going to call me at any moment."

She tenderly smoothed Katherine's hair. "I don't think they are mistaken, sweetheart. I'm quite certain they check and re-check before informing families they have lost a loved one."

By that time, Chris and Ben were in the house. Katherine looked up to see her grandfather standing directly in front of her. He reached down and pulled her to him, embracing her with all the strength he could muster. She cried unabashedly then. As he held her, he fought back tears of his own. All he could think of was the deep love this couple had shared for so long. They had been destined to have a life together and now it had been ripped away. He held her for so long, it was as if time stood still. "We will take you home, my sweet Katie." He could feel her slowly nodding her head in agreement but not saying a word.

Vivian had been quietly talking to Chris and Melanie, telling them that the chaplain and colonel had told Katherine that someone would be in touch with her to help her through the process of planning Captain Kelly's funeral. His remains were required to go through Dover first and then transported to his final resting place. They both thanked her, and she carefully made her way out the door, leaving Katherine with her family.

Melanie slipped upstairs to Jason and Katherine's bedroom. She found suitcases in the walk-in closet and pulled out several outfits, and laid them on the bed. She packed casual clothes and nicer-looking outfits and found shoes to match. She packed her lingerie and nightgowns and then went into the bathroom to gather up whatever she may need in there. She packed as much as she could. Katherine would not be coming back here to live. Before turning off the closet light, she walked to where Jason's clothes were hanging. She gently trailed her fingers down the sleeves of several shirts as tears slid gently down her cheeks. She could smell him here. She went into the bathroom once more and splashed some cold water on her face. She needed to be strong for Katherine.

She headed back down the stairs so they could get Katherine and make the journey home. She felt numb, not looking forward to the days and weeks ahead that Katherine would have to endure.

Chapter Sixteen

They arrived back at Ben's house late that night. Despite the hour, Regina and Dan were waiting for them. When Katherine entered the house, Regina immediately went wrapping her arms around her, saying, "Oh, Katherine, I am so, so very sorry about Jason." Dan hugged her as well, offering his condolences.

Katherine was exhausted beyond belief. She felt numb and didn't feel she had the strength to do anything. All she wanted to do was sleep and hope to wake up with all of this having been a bad dream. She told everyone she loved them and excused herself as she went up to her room. She didn't even bother to open her suitcases that were on the bench at the foot of her bed and change, but rather just laid down on her bed, covering herself with the quilt her grandmother had made for her when she was a child. She fell asleep holding her locket.

After Katherine was upstairs, Regina went to Melanie and embraced her in a warm hug, having noticed the tears in her eyes as she watched Katherine ascend the stairs. She said through her tears, "Oh, Mama, what are we going to do? This is all so devastating. How am I going to help Katherine?"

"We will all be there for Katherine. It's going to take a lot of time, but she's a strong woman. She will be okay, but we must be patient with her."

"You're so wise, Mama. You're speaking like it comes from personal experience, as though you lost something before."

Regina looked thoughtful, as though she were choosing her words carefully. "We all experience bad things in our lives at some point, Darlin. It's up to us to deal with them and go on."

"I love you, Mama."

"Thank you." There it is again, Melanie thought to herself. Even at a time like this, she could not say the words. Don't hold it against her, she thought to herself; she's doing the best she can.

Melanie and Chris agreed she should probably stay the night along with Sophia so she could be there for Katherine. It would be quite simple to make a makeshift bassinet using one drawer from her dresser.

She opened Katherine's bedroom door across the hall each time she needed to get up to feed Sophia. As far as she could tell, Katherine had not moved since going to bed. Her heart felt so anguished for her. She felt clueless regarding what she should do to help Katherine.

* * *

"Katherine, it's time to get up, baby. You have a lot to do."

Without opening her eyes, she replied, "Oh, Jason, I'm still so tired. You won't believe the nightmares I had last night. I'll get up soon. Kiss me before you leave."

She turned her head in the direction she had heard his voice and waited for his sweet kiss, but it didn't come.

"Jason, are you going to kiss me or what?" She opened her

eyes at that point, realizing where she was. It was not a nightmare. Jason was gone.

She thought to herself *I don't want to be here. I don't want to be anywhere. How am I going to live without him? I don't want to.* Eventually, she pulled herself out of bed and made her way downstairs to make a cup of tea to take out on the porch. The sun was just coming up over the water with warm hues of yellow and orange. On this, the most southern part of the island, it was mostly residential and very quiet. That's what she needed now. She didn't want to be with anyone or talk to anyone. She wanted only to cease to exist with her innermost thoughts of how perfect her life had been with Jason.

Still dressed in her clothes from the day before, she took a walk on the beach after rolling up her pant legs. The house sat back a fair distance from the water but walking barefoot in the dew damp grass toward the sandy path felt good to her.

The path was enclosed with walls of seagrass on either side leading to the beach. They were waving in the light breeze from the ocean as if they were inviting her to come. She went down just shy of the water's edge before she began walking. Her thoughts consumed her and confused her. She didn't feel like the same person she had been yesterday. Her life would be different now. She was different and wondered what type of person she would become. She'd always been so strong and known exactly what she wanted. Now she felt weak and didn't know where to go from here.

She did not know how long she'd been walking but felt tired, so she turned around to head back. In the distance, on the sandy path, she saw Jason standing about halfway through. She ran toward him screaming his name: "Jason, Jason, Jason... I'm right here." As she got closer, he turned and walked away, vanishing into thin air. She just stood there, trying to catch her breath. Had she imagined it? Was Jason still alive? She stood motionless, trying to come to terms with what had just happened. She wanted to think she had not imagined it but knew in her heart that she had. Emotional exhaustion had overcome her. She needed to lie down and rest. As she was ambling back to the house, she gazed over to her right, noticing the guest house. It was set at an angle with a better view of the ocean. She felt comfort there. It was where she and Jason would sneak to when they wanted to be alone and was the place where they had first made love. It was where she wanted to stay now, alone, and away from the hustle and bustle of the main house. It had a kitchenette, so she could still make her tea. She had no desire to cook or even eat. She sent Melanie and Ben a text message letting them know so they would not wonder or worry.

The days that followed were filled with making the arrangements for Jason's funeral. The family support staff from the base had been very helpful in relieving Katherine of many of the details except for things she preferred to be a specific way. She moved through the entire process, feeling nothing but her deep-rooted grief. She had been informed Jason's body would arrive on Friday from Dover, exactly one week after she had received the heartbreaking news.

People from the community came and went, offering their condolences, with many dropping off food. Melanie wanted to do something that might help to lift Katherine's spirits, so on the day a couple of ladies from the church dropped off a large platter of fried chicken; she decided she would make dinner for the family just like Katherine used to do.

Chris and Regina arrived at the same time that afternoon. Melanie had set a beautiful table in the alcove just off the kitchen. They both made their way to the kitchen entrance, stopping dead in their tracks. There stood Melanie, busy at work, with her hair partially pulled back in a clip, with strands that had come undone and were falling around her face. Her apron was covered in flour, as were her face and the entire center island. The kitchen sink was filled with dirty pots and dishes she had been using.

"Good God, Mel, what happened in here?" Chris exclaimed.

"Hi, y'all. Supper's just about ready. Hope you're hungry."

"It smells awfully good, sweetheart," Regina said, trying to veil her horror as she looked at the sight in the kitchen.

They all sat down at the table a few minutes later, including Katherine, who had agreed to join them. Melanie had prepared mashed potatoes, collards, and biscuits. At least she had intended for them to be biscuits. They turned out looking like round pieces of pita bread.

They made small talk in an effort to lighten the mood.

"Dad, it looks like you've finally hired yourself some help around here," Dan said

"Yes, son. He's a nice young fellow raised close to here. I've known his father for years. He has a good work ethic, and Lord knows I can't keep up with this place anymore at my age."

Chris interrupted the exchange. "Are collards supposed to be crunchy?"

Regina, trying to go to her daughter's rescue, said, "Perhaps you could have soaked them longer, honey."

Melanie looked at her plate, confused, then at Chris and her mother, "I was supposed to soak em?"

They all chuckled. "Well, of course you are. If not, you don't, you can't get all the grit off. Isn't that right, Katherine?" Regina asked.

Katherine, who had only picked at her plate, looked at Melanie and said, "Thanks for doing all of this, Mel."

Ben spoke up, saying, "Now you all leave Melanie alone. It all tastes wonderful, sweetheart."

After dinner, Katherine excused herself, wanting only to go back to the guest house.

Regina offered to help Melanie clean up. Tomorrow was going to be a very hard day for all of them, especially Katherine. Jason's remains were scheduled to arrive.

Chapter Seventeen

Forty minutes before landing at the Charleston International Airport, the Delta pilot announced; "Ladies and gentlemen, I have the distinct honor of carrying precious cargo on board with us today. We are delivering Marine Captain Jason Kelly to his final resting place. Upon landing, we will be met with fire trucks firing a water cannon salute to honor him. I ask that everyone remain seated when we reach the gate so his honor guard can depart first."

They did as they were asked. When they pulled to a stop at the gate, no one moved. You could have heard a pin drop. It was so quiet. Two Marines in dress blues stood from the back made their way up the aisle, and departed the plane.

They escorted the family from the waiting area to the cargo hold of the plane. Melanie had her arm around Katherine's shoulder to steady her as they approached. The honor guard was saluting as the flag-draped coffin was removed from the plane. Even the ground crew had stopped what they were doing and saluted.

Passengers in the terminal had gathered along the

windows in a rush to go nowhere, as they normally would
have been doing, but rather stood and watched the ceremonial
actions take place. When they saw what they assumed was the
deceased's widow walk forward and put her hand on the
casket, they felt humbled, with a lump in their throats.

Dan and Chris had both taken their cars to the airport.
They were following the hearse to the chapel where two
Marines would stay with and guard the casket twenty-four
hours a day until he was transported to his final resting place.
The funeral was scheduled for 11:00 the next morning.
Katherine told the others that she wanted to be with him
alone and they obliged her. Not having heard from her,
Melanie went back to the chapel later that evening. She discovered Katherine curled up on the floor in front of the casket,
sleeping. It truly broke her heart, but she hoped that maybe
this might help Katherine say her last goodbye. She went back
to her car and retrieved a blanket they often kept in the trunk
for when they went to the beach. She used it to cover
Katherine and nodded at the Marines standing guard as she
left.

After the service the next day, the procession headed down
Middle Street toward the cemetery. The flag-draped coffin was
on a horse-drawn caisson. People came out of the shops and
restaurants and were lined up and down the block. Members
of the police force and many others from the community
saluted as it passed by.

* * *

With each rifle volley fired by the seven-member honor guard
team, Katherine's body shuddered. That sound would stay

with her for all eternity. Following "Taps," the flag had been carefully folded and presented to Katherine. "On behalf of the President of the United States, the United States Marine Corps, and a grateful nation, please accept this flag as a symbol of our appreciation for your husband's honorable and faithful service."

They left the cemetery and went back to Ben's estate, where they would accept guests. Regina had taken care of literally everything. Long tables were set up with food and beverages over where the pear trees were offering shade. She had small tables and chairs delivered and set up that were scattered throughout the area. Katherine accepted all their condolences with gratitude. She had rarely seen so many Marines in one place at one time other than the Marine Corps Ball. The entire platoon must have been there. Some of them told her stories about Jason that made her laugh, but all of them, without a doubt, had the utmost respect for him.

It had been a very long, utterly exhausting day. The guests had all gone, and the others were leaving Katherine alone, sensing that was what she needed and wanted. She had worn a brave face all day, but now just wanted to be by herself. She changed into a pair of terry cloth capris and a t-shirt. She walked out the door of the guest house and headed down toward the beach. The sky was a dark grey, even though it was not nearly time for the sun to set. She guessed it to be early evening. The wind had picked up, and the water was looking angry. There were bolts of lightning far out over the sea.

She sat down on the soft sand and stared up at the grey sky. A light weeping rain had started to fall. "You promised, Jason. You promised you'd be back when you told me good-bye." She lowered her body onto the sand. She closed her eyes. Her salty tears mixed with the light rain that had begun to fall upon her face. She didn't want to live. Surely God would forgive her for wanting to die. The sedative Dr. Bob had insisted she take was affecting her, and she drifted into the deepest sleep she had ever had, finally feeling at peace and ready to join Jason.

His arms were around her, gently lifting her from the sand. He was taking her with him to heaven. She held him tightly, feeling content at last, and then everything went dark.

* * *

When Katherine woke up the following day, she had fully expected to be in heaven with Jason. She was in her bed. Her wet clothes were in a heap on the floor next to the bed, but she still had her bra and panties on. Strange....... she did not remember going to bed. She felt overwhelmed and anxious and in need of a long run.

Going through the clothes Melanie had packed for her in a panic, tossing them to her left and right, she couldn't find what she was looking for. *Shoes, shoes, shoes. Where are my running shoes?*

"Calm down, baby. Look in the back of the car. You should find them there," she heard Jason say.

She turned in the direction where she had heard his voice, and he wasn't there. Frozen to where she was sitting on the floor next to the closet, she curled up in a ball, covered her face with her hands, and sobbed.

The days that followed were much the same as the days before. She would either hear Jason or see him at every turn, but the most paralyzing moment was when she had stopped in a small boutique on Middle Street to try to find a couple of t-shirts to wear when taking her morning run.

Having stepped out of the dressing room, she was going through shirts on a round rack when the sales clerk approached, asking, "May I help you find another size?"

"Usually, the size I have on fits perfectly, but I've lost a lot of weight lately. I think I need a smaller size," Katherine answered.

They were both going through the rack, looking for the smaller size, when Katherine looked up and saw him walk past the door on the sidewalk outside of the shop. She immediately ran out the door, calling for him. "Jason, Jason."

The sales clerk was running behind her. "Miss, oh, miss; you need to pay for the shirt you're wearing."

Katherine didn't look back but kept running until she reached him, grabbing his arm. "Jason!"

The man turned, nearly spilling the coffee he was holding. "Watch it, lady," he retorted.

"Oh, I'm so sorry," she said as tears filled her eyes. "I thought you were someone else."

She followed the sales clerk back into the store and paid for the shirt she wore, not even bothering to find a smaller size. Finally, she gathered her things from the dressing room and left. She sat in her car, feeling like she could barely breathe.

It was at that exact moment that she realized she needed to leave. She saw and felt Jason at every turn. She needed to go someplace where she didn't know anyone... did not have to take care of anyone, and, most importantly, would not see Jason. When she got home, she pulled out her laptop and started researching places that might appeal to her on the East Coast where she could relocate and earn her Ph.D. Finally, Boston became evident to her. Harvard would be her first choice, but If she wasn't accepted, she would apply to other schools. The most important thing was that she needed to escape. There were far too many memories here that involved her life with Jason.

Next, she pulled up housing information. She wanted to find an apartment within walking distance from the school if accepted. She felt a sense of urgency to make this happen immediately. It was as if some threatening being was chasing her. If she could run to Boston, she would leave right now. Her decision was made. Now, all she had to do was tell Melanie.

Chapter Eighteen

"Why Boston? It's so far!"

"I know it is, but easy to get to by plane. But I need to do this, Mel. I need to get as far away from here as I can. Everywhere I go, and everywhere I look, reminds me of Jason."

"You know I hate the idea; I don't have to tell you that—but I understand. What can I do to help you?"

"The biggest thing is, go with me to help pack up the house at the base. I'm going to have movers take the things I need, and the rest is going to storage."

"How soon do you want to do this? It's awfully soon, isn't it?"

"The sooner, the better. I feel like I can't breathe here."

By the end of the following week, Katherine had made all the arrangements. Melanie and Chris followed her to the house to help her pack. Regina had offered to take care of Sophia.

"Are you sure, Mama? She still does not sleep through the night sometimes."

"Of course, I'm sure. She's my granddaughter. I love her,

and your dad and I will enjoy spending time with her. So don't you worry about a single thing."

Melanie felt her heart swell. *My Mama loves my daughter. She actually said the words.*

When Katherine told Ben of her plans, her eyes swelled with tears. She hated to go so far away from him. At least when she was at Camp Lejeune, she was only four hours away. This would feel different, but she could get to him by plane if needed, and Melanie promised she would check in on him.

"I love you so much, Grandpa, but I need to do this. I have to get away from here. I don't know how I will rebuild my life without Jason. I don't know how to live in this world without him, and I don't want to."

"My dear Katie, you do what you need to do. When we lost Elizabeth, I didn't know how I would live without her either, but I have my memories of her, and that keeps me going; not that I still don't have days where I feel sadder than others, but that's part of life."

"But how do I get over the pain and go on from here?"

"Life's a journey, my sweet Katie, some of it good and some not so good. We have to take the good with the bad. What you're feeling now is normal, but you are a strong young woman, and you've always given of yourself to help others. Now is the time to focus on yourself. The answer will come to you, but you must give yourself time. Your life with Jason was extraordinary. The two of you had a bond like nothing I've ever seen. Trust me when I tell you that you will find your way, but it may be a long road. Don't give up on yourself."

"I love you so much, Grandpa. Thank you for always being there for me."

They left on Friday morning, two weeks after Katherine had received the tragic news. She was dreading going back to the house to pack it up. There would be so much of Jason there. She didn't know if she could cope with it. She still had horrible nightmares. She could see Jason and hear him. He would be reaching out to her, but she could never quite reach him.

The closer they got, the greater Katherine's anxiety level grew. Melanie was riding with her, and Chris was following in their car. They were on Highway 24, getting closer, when Katherine suddenly felt a panic attack set in and could not breathe. She pulled off the road, stopping short and shoving the gear into park. She had both hands on the steering wheel, gripping it tightly, panting with her head slightly bent toward her lap. Melanie instinctively knew what was wrong. She jumped out of the passenger side and ran around to Katherine at the driver's side. She spoke soothingly to her as she gently tried to pry her fingers from the wheel. Chris was, by that time, standing right behind her. They tried reassuring her as they guided her to the passenger side.

"It's going to be okay, Kat; Chris and I will be there for you every step of the way." She glanced at Chris with an expression that said she wasn't so sure.

They eventually got back on the highway and, once at the gate, stopped at the visitor's center to get a pass for Chris's car. Katherine's, of course, still had a sticker on it. As they approached the gate, the Marines on guard recognized her car. They saluted as Melanie pulled the car through. It felt pretty touching to Melanie, and Katherine tried to muster up a smile and wave.

They pulled into the driveway of Katherine's house. She just sat and stared at the house. She felt motionless like her body had just gone numb. Oddly, she felt no emotion. It was as if she was on the outside looking in, not being a part of it. She wondered if this was how it would be now, not living and being a part of anything but simply existing. She eventually got out of the car and started toward the door. Once inside, it was as though a bat out of hell had flown into her. She went out to the garage from the hallway door just off the foyer and started bringing in the boxes, tape, and paper the moving company had put in there several days ago. She was moving quickly and didn't want to think about the reason she was doing this or anything else that had happened. She just wanted it done.

At her direction, Chris and Melanie slid furniture into two sections: the section going to her apartment and the one going to storage. While she sorted through everything in the kitchen, she'd asked them both to go up and pack up Jason's clothes. She was donating everything.

Melanie left Chris to finish upstairs and went down to check on Katherine. She was still moving quickly, like a woman on a mission. The things she had pulled out of the kitchen cabinets covered all the countertops. Katherine looked up as she saw Melanie enter the room.

She didn't stop working but spoke over her shoulder, "Everything's been pulled out and sorted. I'm ready to put things in boxes." She had pulled her hair up into a ponytail and gathered and tied her shirt in a knot around her waist. She looked exhausted.

"Why don't we take a break and eat something, Kat? You've been working for hours without stopping."

"I'm not all that hungry, but I'm sure the two of you are. So why don't I run to the sub shop and pick up some sandwiches?"

Melanie was dumbfounded at first, not because she expected Kat to cook for them, but in the past, she would never have suggested picking up fast food. Instead, in a matter of minutes, she could throw together a gourmet meal that looked like she'd spent the entire day preparing it. Besides that, cooking was a part of her soul and something she deeply loved to do.

"Don't be silly. I'll help you while Chris runs out to pick up the sandwiches, but only if you promise me you'll take a break and try to eat a little something."

The sub shop was close to the house, so they started boxing up things in the kitchen while Chris was gone. Melanie reached for the tape to secure a box of dishes while Katherine held the top closed when she spotted a small stack on top of the stove.

"Wait, Kat. We forgot those," she said, pointing to the stack.

"Those go in a different box. All the things over there are going to my apartment. The rest of it is going to storage."

"Kat, there is almost nothing there. As far as I can tell, I have a few plates, utensils, mugs, glasses, and a toaster. That's even less than I have in my kitchen, saying something. Those things would be enough for many people, but not you. So how on earth will you be able to cook?"

Katherine, still sitting on the floor with her hands on the box to be taped up, looked pensive.

"I don't have the desire to cook anymore, Mel. That's something I've always enjoyed doing for others more than myself. I'm alone now. I don't want to take care of anyone anymore. I don't want any relationships. I want to figure out how to carry on."

Melanie went over to where Katherine was and sat on the floor next to her, wrapping her arms around her, and rested her head on her shoulder. "You're still the same person, Kat. You've always been the one that cheered for the underdog, listened to everyone's problems, and helped them. You've always given totally of yourself to others, cooking and other-wise. Just think back on all the times you've helped me! You've been through something devastating, but it does not mean you have to give up a part of yourself."

"That's who I was, who I used to be. So I will not allow myself to get involved in any situations or with anyone again that could lead to experiencing this kind of hurt. It's not worth it to me."

"I'm worried about you driving to Boston alone."

"I'm not. The movers are taking my car. My flight leaves Monday afternoon."

After tearful goodbyes at the airport, Chris and Melanie headed home. Melanie felt so despondent. She didn't know what she was going to do without Kat. She had enjoyed living close enough to get together as often as they wanted. Kat was her rock. She had always been the strong one in their relationship. She was determined to make sure the long distance that would now be between them changed nothing. She also hoped that Kat might eventually return home.

Chapter Nineteen

Katherine had been far away within her memories of her childhood and beyond. It was hard to believe that it had all been so long ago. Hearing her phone ringing brought her out of her reverie.

"Well, hey there, Kat. I've got my flight all set up. I arrive at 3:00 on Thursday."

"I can't wait to see you, Mel. I know it hasn't been all that long since we've seen each other, but I so look forward to our time together. I'll pick you up, but it's going to take a while to get through traffic. That's when rush hour starts around here."

"Oh, who cares? We can chat in the car."

"See you Thursday. Love You."

"Love you more, Kat."

* * *

Katherine was waiting outside the terminal. When she saw Melanie, she started squealing like a little girl. She ran to her, wrapped her arms around her, and gave her a big hug. She looked at the enormous number of suitcases and said, laughing, "Are you planning to move in?"

"Sometimes I wish I could," Melanie replied with gloominess.

Katherine glanced over at Melanie as they were pulling away from the airport. She looked good, but the spark in her face was missing.

"So, tell me. How are things with you and Chris? What did you mean back there about wishing you could move in?"

"Oh, I wasn't being serious. You know me. I always manage to say the wrong thing." She chuckled. "That lame statement would work on a lot of people but not on me. Now, spill the beans."

Melanie rested her head against the headrest with a sigh. "I wish you didn't know me so well. It's not that things are bad between Chris and me; it's just that the magic doesn't seem to be there anymore. We do nothing together with just us anymore. Ever. I know he's tired when he gets home, but even if I try to make a good meal or make myself look pretty, he doesn't even so much as compliment me."

"Okay, let's get one thing straight. You'd look beautiful even if you had a bag over your head."

"I'm probably just being too sensitive. Getting away will probably give me a whole new perspective on things. So, tell me, where are we going to eat? I'm famished."

"I was thinking about my place."

Melanie whipped her head around, looking at Katherine in total disbelief. "What? You mean you're cooking again? When did this start?"

"I've been doing it for a while now. I think it started back when I first met my neighbor, Stewart. He's an older gentleman and so lonely. His wife has Alzheimer's, and he's had to move her to a facility that can take care of her."

"How is it I've never met this, Stewart? What type of work does he do?"

"I think the last time you were here, he was out of town. You'd love him. I know you would. He's a retired airline mechanic and even owns a small plane. He loves to do things with his hands and is quite talented. Anyway, he's been very good to me, and I like how it makes me feel to do little things to improve his life. But, on the other hand, he has some terrible days. I don't know how he does it."

When they got to Katherine's, they made their plates, but rather than sitting at the table, they sat on the floor in front of the fireplace, using the square cocktail table to set their things on. Even though it was summer, Katherine still threw a fake log-in. She loved the ambiance. She always loved her "girl time" with Melanie.... always had.

"So, who are we joining at the Cape? I've read a lot of books based there but have never been there myself."

"The house belongs to my co-worker Olivia's parents. They are filthy stinking rich and will be in Europe, so Olivia invited a small group to celebrate the Fourth. I've never seen the house in person, but Olivia says it's enormous and over-looks Lighthouse Beach. She's also invited others, but I haven't met them."

"I don't care if Satan himself is there. I just want to put my toes in the sand and drink some fruity drinks. I'm not even going to need to unpack my suitcase tonight. I packed an overnight bag with everything I need for tonight and in the morning."

"That was a smart way to do it. I have everything laid out. Just need to put it in a suitcase."

After dinner, giggling, talking, and drinking way too much wine, they both went to bed feeling unbelievably excited. They would leave for their trip to the Cape first thing in the morning.

Melanie was still sleeping when Katherine woke up the following day. That was just as well; she had a couple of things to do before they left. After having some much-needed coffee instead of her regular tea, she grabbed a quick shower and finished packing her things. The only thing left was to take Muffin and his needs over to Stewart. He had agreed to watch him while she was gone. They had grown quite close, and Stewart seemed to enjoy him. He would be good company for him. She could not help but worry about Stewart. His wife, Abby's health deteriorated more each day. It was unfair that he had been mourning her loss for years. It was one thing to lose a loved one suddenly, but to endure watching them suffer was something else entirely. He was so brave. She loved and admired him.

The hour-and-a-half drive to the Cape was scenic and beautiful. It was a gorgeous day, and they were both looking forward to getting away. Katherine had directions to the house. Olivia would already be there. While traveling down the main street, they could not wait to take some time to shop. The area was so quaint and filled with lots of interesting-looking shops and places to grab something to eat. It was a trendy area. Tourists were everywhere, browsing about.

Just past the tourist area, Katherine slowed down to a crawl. Olivia had told her that the driveway leading to the house could easily be missed. Melanie spotted the house number off to the right on a column covered in stacked stone with a lighthouse lantern.

"Oh my God, Kat. Look at this place. It's massive."

"You're not kidding. A person could get lost in there."

. . .

The long, cobblestone driveway was encased with massive hydrangeas on both sides leading to the house. There was a circular driveway in front with a large dolphin fountain in the center, surrounded by a large array of colorful flowers. The house itself was enormous but charming from the outside. It was white with black shutters and looked to have a three-car garage attached to one side in an L shape. There were three dormer windows on top of it, making it look like another wing of the house. The house and grounds almost looked historic, being so meticulously manicured.

Olivia heard the car pull up and went onto the porch to greet them. She looked much like she always did, with heavy makeup, hair perfectly done, hot pink nail polish and lipstick, dressed in short shorts and a tank top. She was so innocent, having no idea that she could, at times, look a little cheap but sweeter than a chocolate chip cookie. She was grinning from ear to ear and waving, "Hi, y'all. Glad you could find the place. Let me come and help you with your things."

Katherine introduced Olivia to Melanie as they headed into the house. She told them to leave their things in the foyer while she showed them around, so they could pick the rooms they wanted. They started with the downstairs, moving to a room to their left, which was the family room. The floor plan was extremely open, with windows across the entire back. You could see the water from whatever room you were in. Moving toward the kitchen, double French doors lead out onto a covered porch with enough casual seating for at least two dozen. The view from out there was about as beautiful as it could get. The master bedroom was on the ground floor on the opposite side of the house. Olivia took that room so the others could all be together on the upper floor. The staircase they had seen when they entered the front door must have been fifteen feet from the front of the house. It divided the downstairs into sections with no other walls. Katherine and Melanie picked out side-by-side rooms separated by a bathroom. There was another bathroom across the hall from one bedroom, so they didn't have to share.

At the other end of the hall were three additional bedrooms and two more bathrooms. At the end of that hall was a door leading to a loft over the garage, with room for more sleeping and another private bath. The entire house was decorated with a beach theme. Olivia's mother obviously had collected many things over the years and clearly loved the beach. Yet, with all the grandeur, the house and furnishings were more comfortable and inviting.

After Katherine and Melanie settled, they went back downstairs to find Olivia.

"Olivia, this place is amazing. Thank you so much for inviting us!"

"I'm so glad you could make it, Katherine– and you too, Melanie. Please make yourselves right at home. Let's go to the kitchen and make some drinks. It's five o'clock somewhere," she said, laughing. "The other girls should be here soon."

They made a pitcher of margaritas and took them out onto the porch overlooking the water. The sky was a deep blue and was shimmering on the water. It was such a serene place to sit. The three sat and chatted for a while. Melanie was getting to know Olivia, and they seemed to hit it off. She was an extremely comfortable person to be with. Then, suddenly, she jumped up from the chair she had been sitting in and ran off the porch in sheer delight. She ran toward an older woman crossing the lawn from the house next door.

"Mildred. Oh, my God, it's so good to see you! Come meet my friends."

"Oh, sweetie, I didn't come to stay. Your mother told me you would be coming, so I made you those blueberry muffins you like. I made extra so you would have plenty to share."

"That's so sweet of you. My mouth is watering already. I'd like to introduce you if you're not in a hurry."

"Well, okay, but I won't stay long. You young things don't need an old woman barging in on your fun."

"Don't be ridiculous. You could never barge in. Come, sit and relax with us for a while."

She finally relented, knowing she would not win. Olivia went to make her an iced tea with lemon, knowing how much she liked it. She had known Mildred since she was young, long before she lost her husband and became a widow. She was the motherly type and very kind. She'd always felt somewhat like a grandmother to Olivia. Katherine and Melanie thoroughly enjoyed Mildred. She was one of those people you felt you'd known all your life upon meeting her. She was fun and had interesting stories to tell about the area.

"Olivia, I saw a market on the way here not far away. So, I thought I'd pick something we could make for dinner."

"Oh, no, Katherine. That's unnecessary. My mama stocked the kitchen and freezer for us before she left. I took out a tenderloin I thought we could cook for tonight on the Jenn Air Grill and use the leftovers for sandwiches to take to the beach over the next several days. Mildred, you must stay and eat with us. Please say you will," Olivia pleaded, holding her hands under her chin as if praying. Katherine and Melanie chimed in, agreeing with Olivia.

Mildred was laughing now. "You girls certainly know how to twist someone's arm. Okay, I'll stay, but only if you agree to let me help prepare the meal– and I'm leaving right after dinner. No arguments. I refuse to cramp your style."

Now they were all laughing. Melanie looked at Katherine with a beseeching look. "Kat, if I get everything we need, will you help me make biscuits? The last time I tried, they didn't turn out so well."

Now Katherine was laughing. "I think I vaguely

remember those biscuits. I know you tried your best, but they were just a little flat."

"A little... they looked like tiny flying saucers," Melanie said, chuckling

Just then, the doorbell rang. Olivia got up to answer it. "That's probably the others. I'll be right back."

She came back, followed by two other ladies. She introduced them to the others. Their names were Jane and Tess. Jane had short brown hair and looked to be about thirty-five. She was married with a son and a daughter and worked as a nurse in a doctor's office. She was pleasant and easygoing. Tess was divorced and worked as a real estate agent. She was the exact opposite of Jane. She had shoulder-length jet-black hair and a body that women would pay to have. She was flamboyant, and the way she dressed left little to the imagination. Katherine offered to make another pitcher of margaritas and bring out glasses for Jane and Tess.

While there, she spotted fresh strawberries, grapes, and sliced cheese in the refrigerator. Olivia's mother had gone out of her way to ensure they had everything they needed. She put everything on a dolphin-shaped platter she saw and found some crackers in the pantry. She also noticed that she would have what she and Melanie would need to make the biscuits, including the buttermilk. She had never seen a kitchen stocked so well. Olivia's mother must like to cook. With her tray complete, she went back out to join the others. They all sat enjoying their drinks and snacks for at least another hour, and then Olivia said she would go in and start putting dinner together.

"Not without me," Mildred said. "Remember our deal. I'm coming with you."

Katherine looked over at Melanie, who had been carrying on a conversation with Jane. They seemed to have a lot in common. Tess had been on her phone the entire time. "Mel,

I'm going to go in and pull out what we need to make the biscuits. You stay here and talk to Jane. I can teach you another time."

"Only if you promise, Kat. I really want to learn how to make them the right way," she said, smiling.

Katherine joined Olivia and Mildred, who were already working hard in the kitchen. Olivia had the tenderloin searing on the grill, and Mildred washed and chopped vegetables. Katherine pulled out what she needed and started on the biscuits. The kitchen, like the rest of the house, was massive. There was more than enough space on the center island for all of them to work simultaneously and talk while working.

Olivia had gone out to check on the others, leaving Mildred and Katherine alone.

"That's a beautiful locket you have on, Katherine."

"Thank you. It was my grandmother's. She gave it to me on my wedding day." As soon as the words came out of her mouth, she regretted them. That was a time in her past she didn't share with anyone.

Mildred looked at her thoughtfully. She didn't press any further but knew by the shadowed look on Katherine's face that something was there. She wished she knew. Someone as young as Katherine should be happy. She would love to be able to help her but first needed to know what the mystery was.

Chapter Twenty

They had dinner on the terrace off the dining room. The early evening was warm but not humid. There was a refreshing calm breeze in the air, and smelling the sea breeze was a little slice of heaven. They had all been chatting, and then Mildred decided to do a little exploring.

"When my husband was alive, we would eat outside whenever it was possible. Why close yourself up inside walls when you could sit outside and enjoy all of this? We never tired of the view."

That got Katherine's attention just the way Mildred thought it would. She looked pensively at Mildred before saying, "I'm sorry to hear that. When did your husband die?"

"That was many years ago. He inherited his father's heart; God rest his soul. It just finally gave out on him. But I cherish the many years we had together and have the memories that have allowed me to carry on."

"How did you learn to do that, Mildred? Wasn't it hard to let go and get over it?"

"You never get over something like that, Katherine, but time heals all wounds if you allow it. I had to open myself up to change and learn to do things differently... to live differently with other goals in mind. Being married, I think, is much like a habit. You don't break habits; you replace them with new ones. Of course, that applies to many things other than marriage."

Laughing, Tess broke into the conversation, saying, "My ex-husband was a terrible habit. I'm sure glad I broke that one."

Mildred looked at Tess with a blank expression. She was annoyed that Tess had made light of what she was trying to convey for Katherine's benefit. There was an awkward silence.

Suddenly Olivia spoke up, "Hey, y'all, I have an idea. The Fourth is the day after tomorrow. Why don't we have a cookout and invite some of our neighbors? It's been a tradition we've done many times over the years. So, Mildred, what do you think?"

"I think that sounds like a lovely idea, Olivia. I know a lot of people will come. We could ask everyone to bring a dish to share."

"Oh, this is going to be so much fun! First thing tomorrow, I'm going to start making plans."

Everyone did their own thing after dinner. Jane and Tess wanted to take a walk on the beach, and Melanie wanted to call and talk to Sophie and then soak in that exceptional tub in her bathroom. Mildred thanked Olivia for inviting her to dinner. She spoke to all the others and then strode across the lawn back to her own house.

Katherine could not get Mildred's words out of her head. She knew she had not been brave after Jason's death and lived in fear. She had not allowed herself to get close to anyone in years, and forming a new relationship with a man was the furthest thing from her mind. She knew she needed to change but didn't want to think about it tonight. Twilight was falling, and she really wanted to pour herself a glass of wine, sit outside, and listen to the night sounds. Tomorrow was another day. She would give more thought to her life in the morning.

The house was quiet when she woke up early the following day, with the others still sleeping. She crept downstairs so as not to wake anyone. The cool morning air was drifting through the open windows. She made her way into the kitchen to put on a pot of coffee for the others and made herself a cup of tea. She went out to the terrace and settled into an oversized chair, folding her legs beneath her. She was in awe at the beauty of this place.

The lawn was large, with a panoramic view of the ocean and perfectly placed hydrangeas in various colors. It looked like it could have been a mural and not real. The clouds drifting high in the sky were making way for a beautiful day to spend on the beach. She knew Melanie would want to go, and maybe the others would, too. After a while, she took her tea and ventured down to the beach. The calm sea and the small waves lapping at the sand as they came in made her feel incredibly relaxed. She walked to the water's edge, letting the warm water make its way over her feet. The dolphins had appeared. They were majestic creatures she could sit, watch, swim, and play all day. They seemed to notice her standing there, pushing their upper bodies out of the water and waving their heads at her as if they wanted her to join them. She laughed out loud despite herself. She backed away from the water and found a dry place to sit in the soft sand. The morning sun felt so good as it fell on her face. She closed her eyes slightly, tilting her head up toward the sky. What Mildred had said last night crept back into her thoughts. She needed to live life differently, but how? She drew her knees toward her chest, wrapped her arms around them, and rested her forehead on them.

Haven't I lived life differently? I moved to a different place. No, Kat, you fled to a different place to escape the memo-

ries, but aren't they still there? Yes, they are. I'm still living in fear, not wanting to get close to anyone, so I'll never feel that kind of pain again. I don't even stay at Grandpa's when I go for visits. I stay with Mel and Chris. I have friends, don't I? No, I don't. I don't refer to anyone I know as a friend. It's too dangerous. I have acquaintances and keep them at arm's length. I've gotten close to Stewart, but that feels different. He needs me, but I think I may need him too. He's being brave as his wife is dying before his eyes. I need to come up with a plan. Besides Jason, I need to remember things that used to make me happy. That's what I'm going to do. It's time to start living and not just existing. Mildred seems very wise. Maybe I'll talk to her some more.

She raised her head and scanned the horizon, looking for the dolphins again, but they were gone. She took a deep breath, realizing she suddenly felt better. Even though she didn't know her plan, she was determined to come up with one. The others were probably awake by now, so she returned to the house feeling less weighted.

When she returned, Melanie and Jane were in the kitchen having coffee at the table that looked out over the terrace. She went to the refrigerator and started pulling out things she could cook for breakfast. She decided on bacon and cheese omelets and the blueberry muffins Mildred had brought over the night before.

Melanie felt as though her heart was going to explode with happiness, watching Katherine do what she had always done, making a gourmet breakfast for everyone and enjoying it. The enticing smell filled the house, calling to the others. Before Katherine knew it, Olivia and Tess were in the kitchen too.

"It smells incredible in here, Katherine, and those omelets look so pretty," Olivia said, "I don't think I've ever eaten anything you've cooked before, other than those delightful biscuits you made last night. I can't wait to try all of this."

"It will be ready in just a couple of minutes. I hope everyone's hungry."

Olivia went to grab some plates, silverware, and napkins. The others joined in to help distribute everything as Katherine walked over to set a large plate of food on the lazy Susan in the center. She had also made fresh-squeezed orange juice that she put on the table. They practically ate in silence, devouring the food with each one of them exclaiming to Katherine how heavenly everything tasted.

Melanie spoke up toward the end of the meal, saying, "I've got an idea. Why don't we take turns deciding what we want for dinner, picking up whatever is needed, and letting Katherine cook it?"

Katherine was laughing. "Even though I know you're kidding, I'd be happy to do that. You know how I've always loved cooking."

Jane said, "I like that idea, and the rest of us can do all the cleaning up. Katherine shouldn't have to cook and clean."

The rest of the girls looked at Jane and then back at Katherine.

"I'm not kidding. So, ladies, lift your glasses in a toast to our resident chef." Of course, they broke out in laughter afterward.

While cleaning up, they talked about their plans for the day. Jane and Tess wanted to go shopping to pick something to wear for the party. Melanie and Katherine wanted to go down to the beach and read their books, and Olivia was going to hook up with Mildred to discuss the party details and the guest list. They agreed to reassemble later in the afternoon to figure out who was going to do what the next day to get everything ready.

The beach was already getting crowded, and it was only ten thirty. The tide was out, leaving little lagoons of shallow water young children were playing in. There wasn't a cloud in the sky and there was a gentle breeze blowing to keep them cool. Katherine and Melanie set up their chairs the way they always liked to do, facing opposite directions while facing each other, so they could talk about their books as they were reading. Over the years, when they went to the beach, it had become fun to exchange books one or the other had already read, and then they would talk about them as they were reading. When they first settled into their chairs, they were both in amazement at how beautiful lighthouse beach was. Katherine didn't see any of her dolphin friends from earlier in the day.

"So, how's my goddaughter? We haven't had much time to catch up."

"Sophie is the light of my life, Kat, but she keeps me hoping. She is so tenacious. The other day, Chris had fallen asleep on the couch with his mouth open and I caught her trying to take his temperature with the rectal thermometer."

Katherine doubled over in laughter. "I love that little girl so much. I miss her all the time. What about Grandpa and Ruth? How's everything with them?"

Melanie had a disgusted look on her face. "Grandpa is doing well and seems happy, but Ruth is another story entirely. She's good to Grandpa, but there's a side of her I never see when he's around. Like about a month ago, I stopped over to check on him. I went into the house, looking from room to room, and then stepped into his study. I thought he was sitting in his high back leather chair, which was turned away from me going through some of his files in the credenza. I said, 'There you are, Grandpa.' The chair spun around, and it was Ruth, not Grandpa, sitting in the chair. She looked as though I had startled her. She said, 'Don't you knock? You know Melanie, doors were put on houses for a reason.' I told her I'd never knocked on a door to enter my grandparents' house a day in my life and I didn't intend to start now. I'm sure I sounded rude, but she offended me. She then said, 'Well, it's my house now, and I'd prefer that guests knock before just barging in.' I couldn't help myself, Kat, she had my blood boiling then and maybe I shouldn't have but I said, 'Let me inform you that this is not your house, Ruth, it's my grandpa's and eventually it will belong to Katherine as stated in his will. Please tell my grandpa that I stopped by.' Then I left."

"What do you think she was looking for in Grandpa's study?"

"I do not know, but there's just something about that woman that I don't like."

Just then, out of nowhere, a beach ball crashed into Katherine's head and fell on the sand next to her chair. A little girl of about five came running up to retrieve it. Katherine reached down to pick up the ball to hand it to her. "Hi, there. Is this your ball?"

"Yes. My name is Becky. What's your name?"

"My name is Katherine. Nice to meet you, Becky."

Her mother was right behind her, saying, "I'm so sorry. Sometimes this thing has a mind of its own if the wind hits it just right."

"Oh, it's no problem. Don't worry about it. When you go to the beach, you've got to expect certain things to happen."

As they walked away with the mother holding Becky's hand as she spoke to her little girl, Melanie saw the sorrowful look on Katherine's face. "Kat, why don't you just adopt? Lots of single people do that these days. You were born to be a mother. Just look at how you are with Sophie and how much she loves you."

Katherine looked at her with a dumbfounded look on her face. "You know, Mel, I've never even considered that. Jason and I always planned on having children, but once he was gone, I gave up on that dream."

140

"Well, you don't have to. But, I think it's something you should think about."

Katherine quieted, looking back once again at Becky and her mother, laughing and playing in the sand. *Maybe I should. As Mildred said, "Live life a different way."* She decided that once she got back from this trip, she would look into it. There was no harm in at least gathering some information.

Chapter Twenty-One

When Jane and Tess got back from shopping later that afternoon, they overheard Katherine and Melanie talking in the sitting room just off the kitchen. Katherine was saying, "I can't believe he had an affair with the nanny. She's so much younger than he is. I hope his wife finds out and takes him to the cleaners." Jane and Tess set their packages down and joined them.

Jane said, "I was not trying to eavesdrop, but he sounds like a horrible guy."

Melanie and Katherine laughed simultaneously.

"He's not a real person, Jane. Melanie and I love to read books, swap them, and then talk about them with each other. It's something we've been doing for years, kind of like our own private little book club."

Tess then spoke, saying, "Hey, I've got an idea. Why don't we start a book club, meet monthly, and discuss the books? Melanie, we could put you on Skype."

"Olivia could be a big help to us in finding interesting books. I lean on her all the time at work," Katherine said.

Out of her peripheral vision, Katherine noticed Olivia

coming from the kitchen with a platter of fresh fruit, cheese, and crackers just as Tess said, "Shhhhh........ we don't want to include her. She's so backwards and lacks class. I seriously doubt that she even reads books."

Katherine looked at her in total disbelief. "So let me get this straight... you pretend to be her friend. You come to her parents' lovely home for a vacation, eat their food, and drink their wine, and yet you don't want her included in a book club? I think you're the one that lacks class, Tess. I think I'll have to pass on your little club." She left the room fuming, going straight to Olivia, who had turned and walked away, leaving the tray on a table near the space.

Melanie and Jane looked at Tess with their mouths open in stunned expressions. Tess looked back and said, "*What?*"

Melanie said, "Tess, you are such a bitch." She got up and left the room.

Tess looked over at Jane, who was wearing a dark expression on her face, saying, "You agree with them, don't you?"

"Yes, Tess, I'm sorry to say I do. I've never seen this side of you, and I must say it's quite unattractive."

Katherine saw Olivia standing out on the far edge of the Veranda facing the water. She stood beside her, putting her arm around her shoulder. "I'm sorry you had to hear all of that, Olivia."

"Why'd she say those mean things, Katherine? I've never done anything to her."

"She's ignorant, Olivia. Don't give her the time of day. You are a kind, smart person and I'm honored to call you my friend."

"Thanks for sticking up for me in there. Maybe we should form a book club and leave *her* out."

"Oh, I like your way of thinking, Olivia. Why don't you change? I'd like to take you out to dinner with Melanie and me. You deserve it."

Olivia turned and hugged her. "Thank you, Katherine. You're such a sweet person."

They went to Pates on Main Street. They all felt like some good seafood, and the restaurant was known for their desserts. Over a relaxed dinner, Olivia filled them in on the plans for the next day. Mildred had handled most of the planning. Things like that seemed to come second nature to her. They would set up the banquet tables covered with the red, white, and blue tablecloths from prior years that Olivia's Mom had packed away and distribute the food in sections, depending on what category it fell into. Everyone coming was delighted to not only come but bring a dish or dessert to share. In addition, Olivia had asked a friend of hers to set up face painting and games for the children. It was certainly something to look forward to.

Katherine still wanted to talk to Mildred some more to get some guidance but would have plenty of time for that. Thinking of her, however, gave her a sudden light-bulb moment.

"Olivia, I know it's last minute, but would you mind if I invited my friend Stewart? He's my next-door neighbor and an elderly gentleman. I hate to know that he will be alone."

"Of course, Stewart can come. There will be lots of people his age for him to talk to."

* * *

"What about Mr. Muffin?"

"He'll be fine, Stewart. Just leave plenty of dry food and water in his bowl. I've had to do that many times. Please come, I think you'll enjoy it. The people are so nice here."

Stewart agreed to come. Katherine was so excited. She just knew that he would like Mildred and even though he would not form any kind of romantic relationship with her, she

144

would be a good, supportive friend for him. Abby's days were numbered, and she could tell it was weighing on him.

Neighbors started arriving in droves, bringing food, wine, and beer to share. Everyone was in such a festive mood, most of them having attended the parade earlier in the day. The children wore Uncle Sam costumes they had been wearing all day. They loved getting their faces painted while others were racing around, laughing, and playing tag and hide-and-seek. Finally, Stewart arrived, and Katherine walked over to greet him and hug him. "I'm so glad you came, Stewart. Let me introduce you to some of the others." She walked toward Melanie, who was standing with Olivia, Mildred, and other neighbors. She introduced him to Melanie and Olivia first, pointing out that this was her parent's home and that they had graciously given it to all of them to enjoy while they were in Europe. After that, she introduced Mildred to him as the neighbor from next door.

"Stewart, why don't you come get something to eat and a refreshment? There's enough food here to feed an army, and I'd like to introduce you to some of the other neighbors," Mildred said.

Katherine was inwardly glowing. It would be nice for Stewart to spend time with people his age. She turned her attention back to the group she had been standing with when she heard Olivia squealing.

Someone had just run up from behind her, picking her up by the waist and lifting her from the ground. "Hello, gorgeous."

"Eeeeeee. Oh, Whitney, you scared me to death," Olivia said, laughing.

Whitney was a friend Olivia had grown up with. They had been nothing more than friends but had fun together. He was a tall, handsome man with blond hair who was about thirty years old. He was preppy, cocky, and perfectly put together. His parents were quite wealthy and had spoiled him immensely. He rarely worked, and if he did, he worked for his father in his real estate business. He was known in the area to be quite the playboy. After putting Olivia back down and giving her a brotherly hug, she introduced him to the others. He scanned the group with his eyes, landing on Melanie, who was standing just to his left.

"He put his arm around her waist, pulling her closer to him. Well, hello, blue eyes. Where have you been all my life?"

Melanie was looking up at him, smiling like a Cheshire cat.

Katherine was standing across from them. She only had to walk barely forward. She hooked her hand around Melanie's other arm, looking directly at Whitney with a serious-minded, unsmiling look on her face and said, "At home with her husband, raising their daughter" as she was almost pulling Melanie away from the entire group.

Tess had been standing close to them and had overheard the confrontation. Like the snake in the grass she was, she slithered over to Whitney, wrapping her arm around his. "Hi there, handsome. Why don't you and I go take a stroll and find someplace quiet to get acquainted?" Whitney looked at her, noticing the front of her sundress with its plunging neckline practically down to her waist, exposing her voluptuous breasts. "Thanks, sweet cheeks, but I have my eye on something else." He walked away, which made her furious. No one ever turned her down.

Melanie was fuming. When they had gotten far enough away so no one would hear, she shook off Katherine's hold on her. "Why did you do that? You humiliated me!"

"I saved you, Mel. Didn't you realize that guy was hitting on you? You're a married woman, for God's sake."

"I'm also a grown woman, Kat. I can take care of myself. Don't ever do anything like that again!"

They were both angry and went in different directions to

mingle. Katherine noticed that Stewart and Mildred were sitting in the Adirondack chairs under a large shade tree a short way away. She made them each a glass of iced tea with lemon.

"Hi there, you two. I thought you might be thirsty, so I brought you over some iced tea. Are you both having a good time?"

"Oh, we're having a lovely time, Katherine, and the weather has been perfect today," Mildred said

"This is wondaful, Katherine, thank you fowah inviting me. It sure is nice to get out of the city. It's so peaceful heah and the food is very good."

"I'm so glad you're going to stay the night. The guest house is all ready for you."

She heard someone calling her name, so she excused herself. Mildred watched her go.

"I'm going to try to come up with a way to help that poor girl. She is so kind and sweet but is apparently concealing a deep pain within her."

"What is going on, Mildred? Katherine has nevah mentioned anything that was botharing her to me, and I've known her for quite some time."

"I'm not one hundred percent sure, but it's some type of loss. She mentioned to me that the lovely locket she wears was a gift from her grandmother on her wedding day. My guess is something happened to that marriage to end it and she is still living with the grief."

"I didn't know she had evah been married. She nevah mentioned a husband to me during any of owah convasations. If you find out anything, will you call me and let me know? I'll give you my numbah befowah I leave in the morning. I love her as if she's my own daughtah."

"Of course, I will. We can be undercover detectives, so to

147

speak, without letting her know what we're up to," she said, smiling.

* * *

The sun was just going down. Olivia had walked around to the various groups all over the property, suggesting that they make their way down to the beach to watch the fireworks. Whitney had attached himself to the group Melanie had been chatting with but was behaving himself until everyone dispersed, at which point he put his arm around her shoulder and said, "Come on blue eyes, you go with me." Katherine noticed it from where she'd been standing but said nothing this time.

Everyone grabbed blankets from the stack provided or grabbed a canvas chair they could carry by the strap. They all slowly made their way to the wooden path leading to the beach. There was a large crowd of people on the beach already having claimed their spot. There were also vendors selling Italian Ice, waters, and cotton candy for the children. A small group of local musicians had set up back by the dunes and were playing music. Katherine had walked down with Mildred and Stewart, and they were joining some of the other neighbors Mildred's age that she had known for years. The atmosphere was unbelievably festive at this fantastic, family-friendly event. The musicians stopped playing close to nine when the fireworks were supposed to start.

The first ones were just quiet, gigantic, colorful sprays lighting up the sky. Besides, the oohs and *ahhs* children were clapping with delight. They slowly but surely got bigger and bigger and then louder and louder. Katherine suddenly felt she could not catch her breath. That sound she knew she would never forget at Jason's funeral during his twenty-one-gun salute was pounding in her head. She was jumping with each blast. The demons had crept back when she least expected them and paralyzed her. She quickly got up from the blanket she had been sitting on and fled back to the house. She was panting when she got into the house. She shut the door behind her and leaned against it to steady herself. She went to the kitchen sink and splashed cold water on her face. The sounds were still there, getting louder and louder. She raced up the stairs to her room, put her earbuds in her ears, and turned the music up as loud as it would go.

Mildred and Stewart gave each other a knowing look across from where they were sitting. It's as if each knew what the other was thinking. Finally, Mildred excused herself from the others and made her way up to Olivia's house to find Katherine.

Chapter Twenty-Two

When Mildred entered the house, she didn't see Katherine anywhere. She thought to herself that maybe she had gone someplace else. She searched the rooms upstairs just in case. The door to the first bedroom on the right of the stairs was closed. She thought she heard weeping. She knocked, but there was no answer, so she decided to forget her manners and slowly opened the door, peeking in. Katherine was in the center of the bed, hugging a pillow, rocking back and forth. The music she was playing with her phone was so loud she could hear it even though Katherine was wearing EarPods. She gently walked over to Katherine and sat on the edge of the bed, saying nothing but reaching out her arms to her. Then, with Mildred's warmth and comfort, she began to sob. Mildred's heart went out to this young woman. She seemed like a wounded little girl to her. After a few minutes, the crying stopped. Katherine sluggishly pulled away from her. Looking at Mildred's kind face, she said, "How did you know I was upset when I left the fireworks?"

"I have a keen sense of reading people, my dear Katherine,

and my intuition tells me you are sheltering yourself from something very painful."

"The sound the fireworks were making reminded me of a time in my life that haunts me."

From there, she told Mildred everything. The words were flowing out as quickly as a running faucet. She told her about her childhood and being raised by her loving grandparents. She told her about her college years at UVA, about Melanie and their relationship, about Jason being her first and only love. She described in great detail what their life had been like together and how he had become a Marine, just as he had always dreamed of. When she got to the part concerning his death, she took a deep breath before continuing. She remembered it vividly as if it had happened only yesterday. The pain felt so raw, and she paused, often looking at Mildred as if gaining strength to go on. Mildred did not interrupt her, not even once. She listened intently as if there was nothing on Earth more important than this. Katherine shared with her the intense need she felt to run away and try to start a new life in a place where no one would know her and where the demons would not follow. When she was finished, she felt drained of all her energy. She had never shared her past with anyone, not even Stewart. In a small way, sharing it with Mildred had made her feel better.

Mildred reached for a lock of hair and smoothed it back out of Katherine's face. "You poor, sweet child. You have been through so much at such a young age."

"What do I do, Mildred? I've tried to get on with my life— forget the past and the pain and start over."

"My dear, you never forget the past. It's a part of our lives and in some ways has created who we have become."

"But I'm so frightened. I don't want to remember. The memories are just too painful."

"You can't live your life in fear, Katherine. That's not

living at all. You need to face your fears. Treasure your memories, both the good and the bad. Jason lost his life doing what he loved to do. Would he be happy knowing that you have not been able to get on with your life?"

"No... he wouldn't."

"Your dreams can still become a reality, but maybe differently."

"I've been thinking a lot about that the past couple of days. People have always told me I'm strong, but I haven't felt strong at all in a very long time. There was a time I didn't run from any situation, no matter how scary or bad it was. I was always the one picking up the pieces of other people's lives when something bad happened to them. Since I lost Jason, I haven't let myself get close to anyone except for Stewart and, of course, Melanie and my grandpa."

"The strong Katherine is still in there. You just need to create a way for her to come out and shine again. That will happen; I'm sure of it."

Katherine reached out and put her arms around Mildred, hugging her closely just like she used to hug her grandma. "I feel so comfortable with you. You remind me so much of my grandma. Thank you so much for being there for me and for your loving advice."

"I will be there for you anytime you need me. Olivia knows how to get a hold of me, but I'll try to write down my phone number and make sure you get it before you leave. It's been quite a night for you, sweetheart. Why don't you try to get some rest now?"

"I think I will. Thank you again, Mildred."

"No need to thank me. That's what friends are for. However, I do hope you'll consider me your friend. I have a great deal of admiration and respect for you, Katherine. Trust me, my dear, it's all going to work out, you'll see. Now get some rest."

When Katherine woke up the next morning, her eyes felt puffy from crying. That was something she had not done in a very long time. She flung back the comforter, swinging her legs over to sit up on the side of the bed. Her entire body felt like jelly. She had spent much of her energy last night when she shared her past with Mildred. It oddly felt better having done that. She had never talked about Jason with anyone other than Melanie, but that was different. She got up and made her way into the bathroom across the hall to wash her face and brush her hair. She wanted to make sure to see Stewart before he left.

She found him in the kitchen pouring himself a cup of coffee. When he saw her, his face lit up. "Well, good morning, Katherine."

"Good morning, Stewart. Did you sleep well last night?"

"I slept like a rock aftah eating all that delicious food yestahday."

She poured herself a cup of coffee, too. She needed a powerful shot of caffeine today. Then, at her suggestion, they took their mugs outside to the veranda to sit and enjoy the lovely view.

She tucked one leg under as she sat down. Breathing in the fresh morning air, she said, "I don't think I could ever tire of looking at a view like this. It's so peaceful and relaxing."

"Just look at that wotta culla, the way the sun is shining on it."

"I hope you had a good time yesterday."

"Oh, indeed I did. Met a lot of nice people too. I think I might go tell Mildred goodbye befoah I leave. Do you think that would be all right?"

Katherine was secretly overjoyed. Overnight, she had grown to love and appreciate Mildred and thought she would be a good friend for Stewart. "I think she'd be delighted. Even though I just met her as well, I'm very fond of her."

"We had a good convasation yesterday. She's a gracious lady."

They sat and chatted a while longer, and then he said he needed to get going. He wanted to go see Abby on his way home. So he put the duffle bag in his car, and then he and Katherine walked over to Mildred's house. She was in her front yard planting some flowers. She saw them walking over and stood with a warm smile, taking off her gardening gloves to greet them.

Katherine spoke first as she reached out to give her a warm hug. "Good morning, Mildred."

Mildred was looking over Katherine's shoulder and gave Stewart a slight nod of her head and a wink of her eye. "It's so good to see both of you again."

"Stewart is heading home and wanted to tell you goodbye."

He reached out, shaking Mildred's hand and discretely leaving a small piece of paper in her palm. He wanted to make sure she had his number. "It was so nice to meet you, Mildred. I had such a wondahful time with you and the othahs."

"I do hope you'll come back another time, Stewart, and you too, Katherine. We have a lot of festivals and such here during the summer and fall that I know you'd enjoy."

Stewart got in his car after hugging Katherine goodbye. She stood and waved as he drove away. He had asked her to call him when she got home, which she thought was rather funny. Almost like a father would say to his daughter. He had seemed somewhat different to her today, a little quieter than usual. She knew he was living with a heaviness in his heart these days. She hoped he would not have to endure watching Abby suffer and that God would take her quickly when the time came.

She walked back into the house and went to the kitchen. It was all abuzz. Everyone was up, giggling and talking. Tess was in there too, and even she seemed to be in a good mood.

Katherine, Melanie, and Jane mainly had decided to not let her nasty comments from the other day ruin the trip for everyone, but Katherine intended to keep an eye on Olivia. She would not tolerate Tess hurting her again.

"Katherine, we were just looking for you. Where have you been?" Olivia said.

"I went to Mildred's with Stewart. He wanted to tell her goodbye and thank her for introducing him to some of the others their age yesterday. He had a wonderful time, Olivia. Thanks for letting me invite him."

"Oh, that was no bother. He was so sweet and the more the merrier, I always say."

"Why were you guys looking for me? Is something going on?"

"You will not believe this. My friend Whitney has invited all of us to go out on his yacht today. He has an enormous sailboat with staterooms and everything. I told him we'd pack up some of the leftover food from yesterday and bring it with us. He's going to be providing the wine, beer, water, and sodas. He's inviting some of our other friends to come along, too."

Katherine tried to sound enthusiastic, although the last person she had a desire to be around was Whitney. There was something about him that just totally unnerved her. He seemed a little too sure of himself. "That's wonderful, Olivia, and so nice of him. Are you sure it won't be too crowded?"

"Not even close. That thing has multiple decks, with some in the shade and some not, plus it has a nice sitting area inside with large windows and is even air-conditioned. I've been out on it lots of times. You won't believe the beautiful areas he will take us to."

All the others seemed excited about the adventure, so Katherine put on her happy face and faked it. It would not be fair to the others for her to squelch their fun. She went up to quickly change, as did the others, and then she went back down to the kitchen to get the food ready. Katherine packed up some food. She made sandwiches, fruit, crackers, cheese, and even a couple of hoagies using the French bread loaves she found in the freezer. She set them out on the granite to defrost while she was getting everything else ready.

Everyone had come back down except for Tess and were helping to pack everything in coolers that they were taking to contribute. Tess eventually entered the kitchen wearing an extremely small bikini top and a skirt tied around her waist. Melanie was the first to see her.

"Well, HELLO, Tess! Where did you find that gorgeous eyepatch you're wearing as a bathing suit top?" Melanie insulted.

Tess shot her a sarcastic look as the others looked on in complete shock. "I plan to catch a fish today, Melanie."

"Well, I'm pretty sure even fish have to work for their meals. So you better put a lot of sunscreen on those pups, or you'll be bringing back a couple of baked lobsters."

Katherine was standing close enough to Melanie to give her a gentle kick with no one noticing.

"*OUCH!*" Melanie screeched

"I'm sorry, Mel. I didn't realize we were standing so close."

Melanie got her message and said nothing more. Katherine would rather have had a tooth pulled than go out on Whitney's yacht today, and mentally prepared herself for what promised to be a very long day.

Chapter Twenty-Three

When they arrived at the marina, Olivia spotted his yacht immediately. It was called the Majestic and looked like something you'd see on a television show about million-dollar yachts. All the girls were oohing and ahhing when they saw it. They could see Whitney looking like his dapper self, greeting his guests as they boarded. As usual, when he saw Olivia, he gave her an enormous hug, lifting her off the ground because she was so much shorter than he was. It always made her giggle.

Tess gave him an alluring look as she boarded, getting a little too close to him, and said seductively to him, "This is going to be a day we will never forget, Whitney. Then she kissed him directly on the lips. "You and I need to find a way to hook up today. I can make all of your dreams come true."

He rather politely said, "I'm glad you and the others could join us. I think I'm going to be busy today, so maybe some other time."

She gave him a thwarted look as he turned his attention to the others boarding the yacht. He greeted each one individually, telling them welcome aboard and to make themselves at home. When he saw Melanie, his facial expression changed. He reached out, putting his arms around her waist, and kissed her cheek.

"Well, hello, blue eyes. We meet again. I'm so glad you could make it." Melanie was all smiles and Katherine saw it. She could not understand why she was allowing this jerk to flirt with her. It was as though he had cast some type of spell on her. She knew she'd need to keep an eye on her and protect her from his advances.

Once everyone had arrived and Whitney had given everyone a tour, they set sail. They were headed to Jeremy Point Beach, where there was a secluded sand bar. It was high tide, so they could watch the seals playing close to the shore. Whitney anchored the boat so anyone who wanted to go swimming or hop off to explore the beach could do so. Several within the group tossed blankets out on the beach and set up a picnic lunch. Everyone was more or less doing their own thing. Katherine had to admit it was truly relaxing. She and Melanie had been lounging on one deck, where they had taken in the amazing views. The warm sun felt heavenly.

They eventually got back underway and were crossing the harbor toward Great Island. Melanie and Katherine had been mingling with some of the other guests. Everyone was quite enjoyable and so relaxed.

Whitney came up behind Melanie, wrapping his arms around her waist, "Come with me, blue eyes. I want to show you how to steer the boat."

Melanie went with him back to the enormous wheel. He instructed her on exactly what she needed to do and how to make the sails do what she wanted them to do. He was mostly standing right behind her, often reaching around her with his long arms to assist her. She would often tilt her head back so she could see and hear him better. It looked a little too chummy. Katherine had noticed and did not like how this looked.

Tess walked over and stood next to Melanie behind the wheel once when Whitney had briefly stepped away. "Are you having fun, Melanie?"

"I'm having a great time," Melanie said with an enormous grin on her face.

"I wonder how your husband would feel about this great time you're having?"

"My husband is none of your business, Tess," Melanie said as she glared at Tess.

Whitney returned just then, having turned the steering over to one of the other guys he sailed with all the time and suggested to Melanie that they go up to the top deck, where some others were, to better see the natural landscape.

"I think I'll stop in the galley on the way up and make myself a drink," she said.

"You go on up, blue eyes. I'll go make it for you and bring it up. What's your pleasure?"

Melanie giggled. "Something cold and fruity with rum, please." As she was climbing the steps up to the next deck, Whitney gave her a quick, playful pat on her butt. Laughing, he said, "I'll be right up." Then he entered the galley.

Katherine had not taken her eyes off them. She had also noticed that Tess was always nearby, like a cat watching its prey. She obviously had a thing for Whitney and was doing everything she could to catch his attention.

When Katherine saw Whitney enter the galley, she followed shortly behind him so as not to be too obvious. He was at the bar mixing drinks for himself and Melanie. She went to stand directly beside him so that their conversation could not be overheard.

"Stay away from her, Whitney. She's already taken."

"Don't you think that should be up to her, Katherine? Besides, we aren't doing anything wrong. Just having a little fun."

"There are many others here with whom you could have some fun. It does not need to be Melanie."

He looked at her with an evil smirk. "She's the only one I want, Katherine, and I always get what I want." He picked up their drinks and walked away. She couldn't say anything else without causing a scene.

The rest of the day went much the same way. Whitney would not take his eyes from Melanie. It was as though she had become some sort of quest for him. More often than not, there was a large group of others, which Katherine made certain they were a part of. Pretending to laugh and enjoy herself had been exhausting. What had started out to be a delightfully beautiful day on the water had turned into what felt like a full-time job of keeping watch over Melanie. On top of that, Tess had once again tried to pick on Olivia. She was clearly jealous of the close relationship she had with Whitney. In front of everyone, she pointed at Olivia's rather large breasts, saying, "Are those real?"

Olivia seemed stunned but placed her hands over each of her breasts, saying, "What, these? Of course, they're real."

Katherine could not help herself. She looked directly at Tess and said, "How much did you have to pay for yours, Tess?"

Tess scowled at Katherine. There was nothing she could say. Hers were definitely not real. Because of the flimsy way she dressed, you could see the scars. Katherine could not wait for this day to end.

The yacht had turned into a small private cove to anchor and let everyone go swimming. Whitney wasted no time scooping Melanie into his arms and jumping with her into the water. For fear of falling, she'd had little choice but to hold on tight by putting one of her arms around his neck (click). When they landed in the water and came up for air, she was laughing hysterically and splashing water at him, pretending to be angry, but in reality, it had been fun. It was like being a kid again with nothing more to worry about but having fun with friends. By this time, others had jumped into the water too. It felt so refreshing after being in the scorching sun all day. Before Katherine knew what was happening, some guys had gone underwater and were lifting the girls out of the water, so that they were sitting on their shoulders. A guy named Roger had her on his shoulders and, of course, Whitney had Melanie on his. If it had not been for the situation with Whitney and Melanie, she would have enjoyed it. She had not played this game in years. They were all laughing and splashing about, all trying to be the winners. (click, click-click)

They pulled back into the Marina just as the sun was setting. It had started as a yellow ball of fire that had quickly changed to hues of orange and then almost tangerine as it dissolved in the water. Birds flew home across the sky as the sun dropped halfway into the water. Just as they docked, the dusky sky intensified, giving way to a brilliantly star-lit night.

Between the day out on the water, the sun, the drinks, and watching over Melanie, Katherine was exhausted. All she wanted to do was get a hot shower and go to bed. When they arrived back at the house, some wanted to stay up while others were ready for bed. Katherine said goodnight to everyone and thanked and hugged Olivia for the trip again and for such a lovely day. After she took her nice, refreshing shower and put on her moisturizer, she climbed into bed and fell into a deep slumber.

When she woke up the next morning, she felt fully refreshed. Despite her worries about Melanie, it had been an enjoyable day on the water. She couldn't deny that Whitney's yacht was magnificent, and the other guests onboard had been quite enjoyable. With only her long comfy sleeping shirt on, she made her way across the hall to her bathroom. She washed her sun-kissed face from the day before, applied moisturizer, and brushed her teeth. She was looking forward to a relaxing cup of tea. As she exited her bathroom to go find a pair of shorts to put on, she heard Melanie's bedroom door open. It surprised her she was awake so early. Melanie had always liked to sleep in, especially after a day like yesterday. She glanced down the hall toward Melanie's bedroom, only to spot Whitney coming out. Her mouth gaped open. She was in complete shock and at a loss for words.

As he walked toward her, he mimicked, pulling up the zipper to his pants. "I told you, Katherine, I *always* get what I want." He continued to walk away with a devious smirk on his face.

She ventured down to Melanie's bedroom and pushed open the door that was partially ajar. Melanie was sitting up in the bed, the sheet pulled up around her, obviously naked underneath.

Katherine looked at Melanie furiously. "What have you done?"

"I don't know. I hardly remember anything about last night. Jane and I were still sitting outside, talking and having a drink. He stopped by to return a cooler that he thought belonged to us. I offered him a drink. Jane eventually went to bed, so it was just the two of us. I told him it was getting very late, and I was ready to go to bed. When I stood up, I was wobbly, so he steadied me and helped me upstairs. I don't remember anything after that."

Katherine was enraged. "Did Chris or Sophie enter your mind even once last night?"

Melanie was speechless. She didn't know what to say. She must have been drunk when it happened and didn't want to admit that she had not thought of or considered Chris or Sophie at all. She just sat there looking at Katherine, saying nothing.

"I didn't think so. You disgust me!" She stormed out of the room and went to her own.

Melanie had gotten out of bed and had put on some clothes. She hated herself for what she had done, but there was no undoing it. She needed to figure out what to do. As she was going down the hall, passing Katherine's room, she saw her throwing her clothes in a suitcase.

She stood by the doorway. "What are you doing?"

"I'm leaving. That's what I'm doing. I can't bear the sight of you." She never stopped packing as she was talking.

"What about me? How am I going to get back?"

Katherine zipped her suitcase closed, picked it up, and headed out of her bedroom, stopping when she got next to Melanie. "You're a grown woman and can take care of yourself, remember? You figure it out."

Everyone else was still asleep when Katherine left. She decided she would call Olivia later and tell her only that something had come up and she needed to leave. She cried the entire way home. Not only was she immensely disappointed in Melanie, but they had never argued like this. Their relationship felt as if it had been shattered as quickly as a ball flies through a window. She had no idea what would happen next.

Chapter Twenty-Four

While she was unpacking and putting things in the wash or away, everything that happened just a few hours ago drove through her mind like a freight train not able to stop. Words had erupted from her mouth that she never thought she would ever say to Melanie. She had always been a giver, warm and loving. Even as a child, she had been the one that took up for other children that were being picked on. She had never been a judgmental person, but wasn't that what she was doing now,: judging Melanie for her mistake? Could it have been the green-eyed monster of jealousy? that Melanie was willing to throw away what Katherine had lost so suddenly without warning? The morning had dawned with the sweet chirping of the baby birds on the ledge outside of her bedroom window, promising a better day than the day before. Now it felt like a good cup of coffee that had suddenly turned to ice. She knew she had to fix this; she just needed to figure out how.

Stewart had noticed her car pull up and wondered why she was home so soon. Was it possible that he had misunderstood what day she had told him she was coming home? He was sure she would let him know she was home after she got settled and that she'd want to see Muffin. He was going to miss him, though. He'd been such good company in this quiet, lonely house. His phone rang, and he walked over to pick it up. He didn't recognize the number. "Hello."

"Stewart, this is Mildred. Olivia told me just a while ago that Katherine left suddenly this morning before anyone got up. She called her and said something had come up but didn't want to wake anyone. Is everything okay with Abby?"

"Abby's about the same. I just noticed Katherine had gotten home a while ago. I haven't seen her yet but planned to go ovah in a little while."

"Could you do a little detective work and try to find out what happened? It's not that I'm being nosy, and it's certainly none of my business, but I've grown so fond of her in such a short time, and I can't help but worry about her."

"Of course, I will. Yowah numbah showed up on my phone. I'll call you back once I know something."

He ended the call, scratching his chin with his fingers. He wanted as much as Mildred did to know if everything was alright with Katherine, and the sooner the better. He went out back and start making some noise, hoping to get her attention.

She walked through the tall fence gate. "Hi, Stewart. I came back a little early. I've had enough sun and I have some things I wanted to get done around here." She was talking much too fast and knew it. The devil himself would have known that she was lying.

He couldn't help but notice that her eyes were red and swollen. He slightly tilted his head and eyed her with skepticism. He took off his glasses and cleaned them with his shirt, still looking at her. He held them up toward the light of the sky, checking to see if they were clean as he said, "Is that the story yowah going to stick with?" Then he looked back at her.

"It's the one I had planned to stick with, but apparently you know me too well." Still standing in the same spot, she dropped her face into her hands and began to cry again. "Oh, Stewart, I've done a terrible thing."

"I find that hawd to believe. Yowah one of the kindest people I've evah known."

"Melanie and I had a terrible fight, and I said some mean and hurtful things to her. I left abruptly and we haven't spoken since. I didn't even give her a ride home."

He walked over to her and enveloped her in his strong, fatherly arms. "Now, now, Katherine. I'm showah everything is going to be alright."

It was difficult to even understand what she was saying. She was talking through her tears and the words were spilling from her mouth all at the same time, like jellybeans out of a toppled jar. She didn't elaborate on the details because she felt that was private, but she told him as much as she felt she could.

"Come sit down ovah heah and let me go get you a glass of watah." When he came back out with the water, he also had a box of tissues in his hand and handed both to her as he sat down across from her.

She had calmed down just a bit, but lonesome tears still fell from her eyes. She continued to talk, but it was mainly about her guilt over being so cruel and letting her anger and disappointment get the best of her. Stewart patiently listened, nodding his head.

After what seemed like hours, though it had been much less than that, she stood to leave.

"I'm sorry for taking up so much of your time, Stewart, but I can't thank you enough for listening."

He stood and walked over to her and hugged her once again, then with his hands on both of her upper forearms, he said, "As you and your cousin Melanie sort all of this, and I'm showaw you will, I want you to keep this in mind: Patience is a virtue, but fowahgiveness is divine. Love is a strong bond, my dear Katherine. You and Melanie will work all of this out." He then kissed her on the cheek. She followed him into his house to collect Muffin and his belongings and headed back to her place. Once she was gone, Stewart called Mildred to fill her in on what had happened, so she would not worry.

When Katherine went inside, she heard her cell phone chirping with a new text message. It was from Melanie. *I can't begin to tell you how sorry and ashamed I am, Kat. You were right about everything you said. I'm going to catch a ride with Jane and Tess. They are going to drop me off at the airport. I already have my flight scheduled to leave in two days. I need time to figure all of this out and find a way to tell Chris about what happened. Our marriage may not be perfect, but we've always been honest with each other. I'll call you in a few days. I love you more than you know!!!!*

Katherine just stood there holding her phone in her hand. The thing she wanted most to do was call Melanie, but she knew she needed to give her time to sort out her own life, so what she did instead was text her back: *Love you More!!!!*

Katherine felt so burdened over the next couple of days. She had at least taken the time to contact an adoption agency to get information and start filling out the paperwork to adopt. Despite everything else that had been going on, thinking of having a child of her own lightened her spirits. She was feeling more excited than she had felt in years. She had already walked through her house making mental plans for how she would set up her nursery. It didn't matter to her whether she adopted a boy or a girl, she just knew she wanted to be a Mother. If it had not been for Melanie suggesting adoption, it may have never occurred to her. She had given up on having a family when she had lost Jason. She had given up on life other than going through the motions. As much as she had loved Jason and their brief life together, in a peculiar sort of way, she felt she was slowly but surely letting go of the heartbreak and making room for something else; something different.

Katherine went to take the trash out later that day and heard an enormous crash coming from over the fence at Stewart's. She ran over immediately and found Stewart in a drunken stupor, having knocked over a table that had fallen on the patio. She went to help him up.

"Stewart, are you okay?" His speech was unbelievably slurred. She could hardly make out the words he was trying to say. "Aggggg, me Abby, his push, hosche, I mean hostile, is coming." He was half crying but trying to communicate to her what was going on.

"Stewart, are you trying to say hospice has been called in for Abby?"

He lowered his shoulders and was sitting slumped over. He started to sob, then said, "Yes. Me, Abby's going to die."

She knelt in front of him and wrapped her arms around him, holding him tightly with small tears in her eyes. "Oh, Stewart, I'm so sorry. I'll be by your side the entire time and will call anyone you need to let know."

She knew she had to be strong for him. He had been mourning her loss for a long time. This would be the last phase and he would need someone. She made some coffee and something hearty for him to eat. Once she had him sobered up, she drove them both to be with Abby.

They spent the next couple of days at the facility keeping their vigil. Abby's body was shutting down on her. All the Nurses could do at this point was to keep her comfortable. Stewart was doing much better now. He had reached a point of acceptance and would often kneel beside her bed and pray while holding her hand that God would take her soon and not let her suffer. Katherine had taken her briefcase with her paperwork for the adoption so she could work on it when

Stewart would leave the room. He came back in once and saw her working on it.

"That's quite a pile of papahwork you have, Katherine."

She looked at him and smiled. "I've decided I want to adopt a baby, Stewart. These are the papers I need to fill out to get the process started."

He clapped his hands together and smiled for the first time in days. "That's wondahful news, Katherine. You will make an excellent mothah." She looked so beautiful and happy to him. He knew he was walking on thin ice but took the plunge. "Have you evah been married?" The way she looked at him was not one of sadness, but one of trust. She told him everything about Jason that she had shared with Mildred just a few days ago.

"That must have been a very hawd time fowah you."

"Yes, it was. I ran away from where I grew up to start a new life here. I wasn't really living at all until I met you. You inspired me to try to find a way to deal with my grief and do things again that I used to love to do. Mildred encouraged me as well. She also lost the love of her life but found a way to go on without him and have a happy life, even though it is different. Despite everything, I know I have a lot to be thankful for."

"Yowah a fine young woman and strong. I think yowah going to have a wondahful life."

They left after a while longer. The Nursing staff had assured them that the time was not near yet and that they would call if anything changed.

* * *

It was late in the day, and she felt so filled with anxiety over worrying about Stewart and Melanie that she poured herself a glass of wine and took it outside to listen to the katydids in the darkness, with only the light of her kitchen streaming out. She knew that she and Melanie were going to be okay but what about Melanie and Chris? She did not know what Melanie was going to say to him or how he would react. Would this end their marriage? She hoped not. People make mistakes and sometimes they are bad, but she hoped Chris loved Melanie enough to be able to forgive her and work on what had gone wrong in their marriage. Perhaps she could offer to go down and watch Sophie for a while so they could go away together. God only knew when they had been able to have any real time alone together between their jobs and parenting.

Her phone ringing plucked her out of her deep thoughts. "Hi, Grandpa. To what do I owe the honor of getting a call from you at this hour?"

"There's been a terrible accident, my dear Katie. It's Melanie."

Chapter Twenty-Five

After Katherine left, Melanie kept totally to herself. She felt so despondent going for long walks on the beach, thinking about it repeatedly in her head. She couldn't believe she had slept with Whitney and couldn't even remember it, but she knew it had happened. That night, she had felt like she was in a fog, not even feeling in control of herself. She had not had that much to drink, only two gin and tonics. Whitney had offered to go in and make her last one... then it hit her. Whitney must have put something in her drink. She slightly remembered everything until he helped her climb the stairs and then her mind went blank. Oh my God.... He roofied me so he could get what he wanted. He had been flirting with her all day, but they had not done anything that would be considered cheating on her husband. She was just having fun but knew, thinking back, she should have listened to Kat and ignored his advances. God, how she hated herself right now. If she had a gun, she would shoot that son of a bitch! There was no point in going to the authorities. She had no actual proof. What was she going to tell Chris? How could she explain any of this? The bigger question was, would he believe her, and if he did, was he likely to react and go after Whitney himself? One thing she knew for sure: she loved Chris. The last year seemed to have been nothing but problems but they could be fixed.

As soon as she got back to the path leading up to the house, she borrowed Olivia's car and went to find Whitney. She found him in the first place she looked on the dock next to his precious yacht. When he saw her approaching, he stood from what he had been doing with the ropes, smiling. "Well, good morning, blue eyes."

Walking up the dock seething with anger, fists clenched, she connected with his chest. "You put something in my drink the other night, you son of a bitch. What kind of lowlife are you?"

Whitney looked at her sarcastically, laughing. "Now, why would I do that? Besides, you seemed to want it."

"You and I both know that's a damn lie."

The more she punched him, the harder he laughed. "You are even more beautiful when you're angry."

He began slowly backing up to avoid her and lost his balance, falling off the dock into the water. "Hey, blue eyes, toss me a life ring."

Looking down at him splashing about to keep afloat, she said, "You are exactly where you belong, you bottom feeder." She stormed away as quickly as she arrived.

* * *

Melanie was in agony. They were leaving in the morning. Between now and then, she had to figure out how to explain everything that had happened.

She hardly slept that night. She kept having nightmares about Chris's reaction. In some of them, he went into a total rage, and in others, he was quite understanding and said they'd work through it all. One thing was for sure, by tonight, she would know. Her flight would arrive back in Charleston at six o'clock.

When she landed, she sent Chris a text telling him she was going to take an Uber home so he would not have to hassle with Sophie. She had left her car at home when she left so he could look at it because the brakes had been making a squealing noise. She still hadn't come up with the right words. How do you tell your spouse, "Oh, and by the way, I had sex with this guy when I was gone?" She felt so nervous; she was wringing her hands when they pulled into her driveway. She got out of the car, collected her luggage, and sauntered to the front door.

With her hand on the doorknob, she took a deep breath before going in.

"I'm home," she said as cheerfully as she could. She didn't hear or see anyone, so she started making her way through each room downstairs. "Chris, Sophie, where is everybody?"

When she got to the kitchen, she saw why no one answered. There sat Chris at the kitchen table with eight-by-ten color photographs scattered on the tabletop of her and Whitney at the Cape. He didn't even look up at her, even though he knew she was there. Instead, he just stared down at the photos with a despairing look on his face.

"Where did those come from, and where's Sophie?"

He looked at her as though she were insane. "Why does it matter where they came from, Mel? By the looks of them, though, you had yourself a delightful time. I dropped Sophie over at Ben's. She's staying the night."

She had been able to see what the pictures were of even without getting any closer than she was. "Chris, I can explain. It's not what it looks like."

He sat back in the chair, crossing his arms over his chest. "Well, then, why don't you enlighten me? Because it certainly looks like you and this asshole were awfully chummy."

She slowly dropped down in the chair across from him. "He was just some guy. Kat's friend invited some neighbors over to celebrate the Fourth, and he was there. The next day, he invited everyone staying at the house and a bunch of his other friends out on his yacht for the day. It was harmless."

"It doesn't look so harmless to me. Let's take this one, for instance. You are apparently driving the boat and he has his arms around your waist and you're looking back at him. Oh, and then there's this one of his head between your legs holding you up out of the water. Not harmless? How would you feel if you saw pictures of *ME* like this with another woman?" Then he tossed the pictures back onto the table, looking disgusted and miserable all at the same time.

Melanie got up and went over to him, trying to put her arms around him. He shrugged them off. By this time, Melanie was starting to cry. "Chris, I know it looks bad, but those pictures don't show me doing anything wrong if you look at them closely."

"I've looked at them close enough. I wish you'd just disappear and leave me the hell alone."

Melanie looked at him beyond her tears in total disbelief. "You can't mean that. We need to talk about this."

"There's nothing more to talk about." He put his hands under the table and toppled it over, scattering the pictures and anything else that was on it everywhere. "Get away from me!" He was shouting now and there was no calming him down.

She ran out of the room and up the stairs into the bathroom, where she threw up. She flushed the toilet and walked over to the sink to splash some cold water on her face. She was sobbing uncontrollably, unable to catch her breath. She lowered the toilet lid and just sat there holding her face in her hands and cried until she felt there was no water left in her body to make any more tears. She had lost track of time, not having any idea how long she'd been in there. She went back downstairs to see if Chris had calmed down any. When she got back down, she found Chris sitting on the couch, just staring at nothing in front of him. He had poured himself a scotch and the almost-empty bottle sat on the lamp table next to him. She went into the room and sat in a chair across from him.

"Chris, can we please talk?"

He sat stone-faced, saying nothing.

"Chris, please, we need to talk about this. I promise you, there was absolutely nothing going on in those pictures. I don't even know who took them, but it's clear to me that whoever it was wanted to make trouble for me."

It was obvious that he was still incensed with enraged anger. He squeezed the hand that was holding the glass, breaking it into pieces, leaving his hand covered in cuts and blood.

"I told you to leave me alone, Melanie. Now get the hell out of here!" He grabbed the bottle on the table and threw it across the room. It shattered into pieces as it hit the wall.

She didn't know what to do or how to fix this. Tears slid down her face again. She got up, grabbing her purse and keys, and left.

It had started to rain, and it was very dark, with no stars or even the moon to light her way. She drove around for quite a while, not knowing what else to do. She thought about going to her parents' house but didn't want them to know what was going on. Maybe she should just get a room at one of the inns for the night. She was so ashamed. Within just a matter of days, she had done things that would probably end her marriage. She was going to have to live with whatever consequences she got. She wished she could go back in time and change everything. One thing she knew for sure was that she desperately loved Chris and didn't want their marriage to end. She had not known that before she left for her trip but was seeing things in a different light. She had taken what they once had for granted but would not give up without a fight.

Chris heard the doorbell ring but ignored it. He was still drunk from consuming so much scotch earlier. Then, there was hard banging on the door. He stumbled down the stairs and went to answer it. When he opened the door, the police were standing there.

"What can I do you for, officers?" He slurred.

"Are you Christopher Sandston, Melanie Sandston's husband?"

"That would be me. I'm the lucky guy," he answered sarcastically.

"May we come in?"

Chris stood sideways, extending his arm out and ushering them in. They saw the blood on his hand and some on his shirt. Once inside, they immediately noticed the table toppled over, glanced to their left, and saw the broken glass in the family room below the stained wall. They exchanged a suspicious look.

"Mr. Sandston, we are here because there has been an accident. Your wife has been in a car crash. She was partially awake when we got to her and seemed to say, 'Chris, stop' just before she passed out. They have airlifted her to St. Francis Hospital."

Chris looked dumbfounded, backing up and lowering himself to sit on the stairs. He brought his hands up, covering his face, and became hysterical. "Oh, my God Noooo! It's my fault. I did that to her!"

The two officers looked at each other, bemused. The

sergeant spoke, saying, "Mr. Sandston, are you telling me you attempted to kill your wife?"

Chris, still with his hands covering his face, sobbing, appeared to nod his head up and down.

"In that case, you'll need to come with us. You're under arrest for attempted murder."

Chapter Twenty-Six

Katherine sat straight up, holding the phone. "Oh my God, what kind of accident, Grandpa? Is she okay?"

"I don't know all the details. It appears to be serious, Katie. She is in Intensive Care and is in a coma."

"I'll catch the first flight out in the morning."

"There's more. They have arrested Chris for her attempted murder."

"*What?* That's impossible. Chris would *never* hurt Melanie. I'll be there as soon as I can, Grandpa. Please call me if there's any change. I love you, Grandpa."

"I'll be waiting, and I love you too, my dear Katie."

The first thing Katherine did when she hung up the phone was to schedule the earliest flight out in the morning. She ran upstairs to pack. As she was hurriedly pulling out her clothes, what Ben had said kept echoing in her mind. They had arrested Chris for Mel's attempted murder. Why on earth would anyone think for even a split second that Chris would do something like that? It had to be a mistake. She hoped it would all be sorted out by the time she got there.

Before she left town, she needed to make sure Stewart would be taken care of. He had become like family to her, and she could not just desert him at a time like this. She knew it was late but decided to call Mildred after getting her number from Olivia.

"Hello."

"Hi, Mildred. It's Katherine. I'm sorry to be calling you so late."

"Not at all. I was still up watching an old movie. I'm a sucker for those things. Is everything alright, dear?"

"Well, no, not exactly. My cousin Melanie, who you met, has been involved in a serious car accident, and I need to get to South Carolina."

"Oh, my dear, I'm so sorry to hear that. I hope she will be okay."

"Thank you. The other thing is, hospice has been called in for Stewart's wife, Abby, her days are numbered, and I have been sort of looking out for him. He doesn't have anyone else, other than his sister in Pennsylvania, but she can't travel because of her health issues. I know it's asking a lot considering you just met him, but would you be willing to call and check on him while I'm gone?"

"Katherine, I would be honored, and it's no imposition at all. I'll feel him out and if I feel like he might be comfortable with it, I will get a place to stay nearby, so I'll be close, just in case."

"That's a lot for you to do, Mildred. You are incredibly kind. I could tell he was very comfortable with you. If you end up staying in our area, don't pay for a place. You can stay at my place. Stewart lives right next door. I'll call Olivia and see if she can get my cat and take him to her place while I'm gone.

Stewart usually takes care of him when I go away, but I would not consider asking that of him at a time like this."

"Katherine, you need to go and do what you need to do. I'll contact Olivia, and we will work everything out between the two of us. I adore cats, so if I end up staying in your home, I'll take care of the kitty, too."

"I can't thank you enough, Mildred. You are an angel in disguise. I'll text you Stewart's cell phone number. He also has a key to my place."

"That would be perfect, my dear, and don't you worry about a thing. Between Olivia and me, we'll take care of the home front. I hope your cousin Melanie will be okay. I'll keep her in my prayers."

Katherine thanked her again and promised to text her Stewart's number as soon as they hung up. Mildred hadn't let on to her that she already had it and that they were in cahoots to make sure she herself was okay. Funny how life works out sometimes.

* * *

After her plane landed, she hailed a cab and went directly to the hospital. After finding out Melanie's room number in ICU, she headed upstairs, pulling her suitcase on wheels behind her. She was ill-prepared for what she saw when she entered her room. Melanie was unrecognizable. Her head was bandaged; what you could see of a face was black and blue, she had a broken leg and a broken arm. Ben, Regina, and Dan were in the room. There were no sounds except for the monitors and equipment keeping Melanie alive. Regina was the first to see her come in and went to her sobbing.

"Oh Katherine, look at what's happened. Just look at what that monster did to her," Regina said.

Katherine was crying too. She hugged her aunt Regina, her

grandpa, and her uncle Dan and then went to Melanie's bedside. She took Melanie's hand in her own as the tears flowed slowly down. "What are the doctors saying?"

Dan spoke up from where he had been standing on the other side of the bed. "They haven't been able to tell us much so far. They rushed her into surgery when she got here and are still running tests. She has a lot of internal injuries. She's in a coma and there's no way to know how long that will last." He instinctively knew the question she most wanted the answer to. "They do not know whether she will pull through."

Katherine sunk into a chair next to the bed. Ben came up behind her and laid his hand on her shoulder. She heard her aunt Regina start to quietly cry again. As she touched Melanie's hand, being careful not to disturb the IV, she said almost in a whisper, "Don't leave me, Mel. Stay strong and fight to come back to us. We all love and need you." She stayed like that for a very long time and then stood and asked Ben to go out into the hallway with her.

"Grandpa, are there any more details concerning Chris? I know for a fact he would never have done this or had anything to do with it."

"The investigation is going to take a while. Russell has a good relationship with the police force and has been checking into things."

"I'm sorry, who's Russell?"

"He's my caretaker at the ranch. Haven't the two of you ever met?"

"No, I can't remember that I have, but then I haven't been back to the ranch all that often since... she trailed off. I've been staying with Melanie and Chris the times I've come back to visit. So, what has Russell been able to find out so far?"

"Her car crashed. That much we know, but what they don't know is what caused the car to crash. There does not appear to have been any other vehicles involved. It was raining, so she could have just lost control. That's one theory, but the police seem to think there is more to it."

"What about Chris? What's he saying happened, and why do they think he tried to kill her?"

"He has not spoken one word since he was arrested. He appears to be in shock. They have him on suicide watch."

"I'm going to go see him tomorrow. Maybe he'll open up to me. What about his parents? I assume they've been told."

"They will arrive late tonight or tomorrow. They've had flight delays due to weather."

"Who is watching Sophie? She's bound to be so confused."

"She's at home with Ruthie. She seems oblivious that anything unusual is going on. Chris called and asked if he could drop her off around lunchtime yesterday. Of course, we said yes. She's such a sweet child. When you and I head home tonight, I think we need to stop and pick up some extra clothes for her. Chris didn't bring much. He seemed quite distracted when I saw him, not his usual self. It felt to me as though he had something on his mind."

They went back into Melanie's room and stayed for several hours. Regina had not left her bedside the entire time. She was grief-stricken looking at Melanie. Katherine hugged her when they left and asked her to call if Melanie's condition changed. Katherine offered to drive. Ben looked so weak and tired. She worried about him and his heart condition.

"Grandpa, are you taking your medicine the way you're supposed to?"

"Oh, yes, indeed. Ruthie practically chases me down with the pill bottle in her hand. She's a kind woman, Katie, and she takes good care of me. I know she's not your grandmother, but she is a good companion."

"I'm happy for you, Grandpa, and that you're not alone." And she meant it. She knew what it felt like firsthand and didn't want that for him. Before too long, she would not be alone anymore. She would have her baby and that gave her temporary happiness.

When they got to Chris and Melanie's house, Katherine told Ben to wait in the car while she ran in to grab some of Sophie's things. She used the key Melanie had given her long ago to get in. When she went in, she was stunned. There was broken glass everywhere. The table in the kitchen was toppled over and there were papers all over the floor. She walked over to pick them up and then realized what they were. *Oh, my God.* Pictures of Melanie and Whitney at the Cape. The way these were taken, it appeared that they were alone. Even when they were all playing the game in the water, they only showed Whitney and Melanie. *Oh, this is not good. By the way the house looks, Chris apparently had gone into a rage and, in all honesty, given the way the pictures looked, I understand. I've got to go talk to him tomorrow.* She picked up all the pictures and the FedEx envelope they had apparently come in and went upstairs to Sophie's room and gathered some of her clothes. Her teddy was lying on her bed. She went nowhere without it. Chris wouldn't have forgotten that unless he was REALLY upset.

When they pulled up to Ben's house and around back where they always parked in front of the garages, Ruth was sitting on the porch and Sophie was standing right next to her, staring at what she was doing. When she heard the car doors, she turned and looked and then rushed off the porch directly to Katherine, exclaiming in an excited voice, "Auntie, Auntie!!!"

Katherine scooped her up in her arms. "Hi there, baby girl. I've missed you so much! What have you been up to?"

"Miss Ruthie is teaching me how to knit."

"Oh, that sounds like lots of fun!"

Ruth had gotten up and was walking toward them.

Katherine put Sophie down and she immediately took off running back to the porch to gather her knitting to show Katherine.

When Ruth got to Katherine, she put her arms around her. "I'm so very sorry about Melanie, Katherine. We are all keeping her in our prayers. Has her condition changed?"

"No, it's still the same, but the longer she holds on, I'm hoping is a good thing, but I just don't know."

Ben had pulled Katherine's suitcase and Sophie's things out of the car while all of this was happening. Katherine went over to help him. An idea occurred to her as they were all walking toward the porch. "Grandpa, would you introduce me to Russell tomorrow?" He might be able to help her find out who sent those pictures, since Ben had told her he had a good relationship with the police. She'd take care of that in the morning before going back to the hospital to check on Melanie, but she needed to talk to Chris.

Chapter Twenty-Seven

They all went into the house. Sophie was her usual animated self, talking non-stop. Having Katherine there made it even worse. She loved her auntie dearly, and they had an extraordinary bond. She followed them upstairs to Katherine's bedroom.

On their way up, Ruth said, "I got your room already for ya, clean sheets and all, and there are fresh towels in the bathroom."

Sophie scurried back downstairs to get her teddy. She noticed it right away when they were unloading the car.

"Thank you so much, Ruth. I didn't mean to cause you any trouble. I'll be fine with anything. I know where everything is in this house, so you won't need to bother with me." When they went through the doorway into her room, she immediately noticed that it had been re-decorated. "Where's my quilt?"

"That ratty old thing. I got rid of it and picked out something nicer."

"My grandma made me that quilt." She felt like she could

just cry. That quilt had been made with scraps from the dresses she had worn as a little girl.

"Well, I didn't know about all of that. It looked like something that had seen better days to me. On another subject, I heard you ask Ben to introduce you to Russell. Be careful of him. I don't trust him."

"Why is that?"

"I can't put my finger on it exactly. He's quiet and keeps mostly to himself, but it feels like he's always watching. He lives out in the apartment over the garages now. I told Ben I didn't like the idea of a stranger living on the property, but he didn't agree with me. He's in and out of this house all the time, and things have started to go missing."

"What kind of things?"

"Little things mostly, but expensive. A special vase of mine, a figurine that was on the mantel, silver from the China cabinet..... stuff like that."

"Have you mentioned any of this to Grandpa?"

"Yeah, I did, but he thinks the world of him and doesn't think he would take anything. Says he's like a son to him. He thinks they just got misplaced, and I can't convince him otherwise."

"I'll keep what you said in mind. Grandpa's usually an excellent judge of character, though."

"Well, I'll leave you to get settled. Let me know if you need anything, and there are some leftovers in the refrigerator from dinner. Didn't know what time ya'll would be back, so I made some cold-cut sandwiches and potato salad."

"Thanks. I'll probably take a hot shower, spend time with Sophie, and go to bed early. I'm sure she will want to sleep in my bed with me. She always does," she said, chuckling.

"Auntie, will you read me a story?"

"Of course I will, baby girl, but then we need to go to sleep, okay?"

"Okay," she said sleepily. She was already getting tired. It was way past her bedtime.

Sophie was sleeping peacefully. She had fallen asleep in Katherine's arms before she even finished reading the story. Katherine was beyond tired but just tossed and turned. There was so much going through her mind. Fear for Melanie and then the situation with Chris. She needed to get to the bottom of what happened. The clock on the bedside table read 12:45. She finally went downstairs and made herself a cup of the herbal tea she had brought to help soothe her nerves and bring on much-needed sleep. She had remembered to pack her robe but had forgotten her slippers. She looked in the closet, and the only thing she could find to put on was her bunny slippers, hidden way in the back from when she was a young girl. They still fit, so she put them on and headed downstairs. The house was dark, but she could maneuver her way through by memory without even opening her eyes. She almost tripped and fell when she reached the bottom of the stairs just off the kitchen. There was a rug there that had never been there before. When she entered the kitchen, she stopped abruptly when she saw him going through the drawers. It was the same man she had noticed from across the room when Ben and Ruth married. She knew it was the same man because she remembered the scar above his left eye.

"How'd you get in here?" she asked in an entirely unfriendly manner. She also noticed he was wearing a pistol in a shoulder holster, which made her feel uncomfortable.

"Katherine, that would be with a key." He hadn't liked the way she had practically attacked him and the snippy way she had spoken.

"How do you know my name?"

"I've been around here for a long time. I've always known who you are because Ben always talks about you."

"Why are you in our kitchen?"

187

"I needed to borrow a can opener because mine is broken. Ben and I have an understanding that I can help myself to whatever I ever need. Don't worry, I'll be returning it if that's what you're worried about." He reached the door, opened it, and stopped to look back at her before leaving. "By the way... nice shoes," he said, smirking, and shut the door behind him.

She looked down at her feet, remembering the bunny slippers she had on, and rolled her eyes. With a furrowed brow, she looked back up at the door, thinking, *Why would someone need to borrow a can opener at this hour?* She made her tea and took it back up to her bedroom to rock in her rocker until she felt like she could fall asleep.

When she woke up the next morning, she still felt tired but knew it had to be from the stress of the day before. Sophie was already awake, and she could hear her chattering downstairs and laughing with Ruth. They seemed to get along well. She took a quick shower and got dressed. On her way downstairs, she grabbed the FedEx envelope, took the pictures out, and put them safely in her suitcase.

When she entered the kitchen, Sophie sat at the table eating pancakes. She bent over to kiss the top of her head. "You smell delicious, like maple syrup. I could just eat you up." Sophie squirmed in her chair, laughing hysterically.

After pouring a cup of coffee so as not to bother Ruth by asking if there was tea, she went out onto the porch, sitting down in the rocker next to Ben's, with Sophie tagging along behind her.

"Good morning, Grandpa."

"Good morning, Katie. Did you sleep well?"

"I wish I could say yes, but I had a lot of trouble falling asleep. I kept thinking about things I had on my mind. Hopefully, today will be a better day."

"Yes, I'm hoping for the same. Perhaps you and I could go

check on those things together." They were talking in code, for Sophie's sake.

She could see from where she sat that the lights in the garage apartment were on.

"Grandpa, could you keep Sophie with you for a while? There's something I need to take care of."

"There's nothing I would like better. I'm sure she has plenty to talk to me about." Sophie *always* had plenty to talk about.

It would generally have been too early to knock on most people's doors, but this was important. It couldn't wait. She climbed the stairs up to the apartment and knocked softly. Within seconds, the door opened, with Russ standing on the other side, holding a cup of coffee. He looked like he'd already been up for a while. He was showered and dressed in jeans and a t-shirt. He had jet-black straight hair, and although he was freshly shaven, he had a blue beard. She had always found that attractive in a man, but not this one.

"Well, we meet again. Oh, and by the way, my name is Russ."

"I'm sorry to knock on your door so early, Russ, but there's something important I need to talk to you about."

"Of course, please come in. Is everything okay with Ben?" As she walked past him, she couldn't help but notice how good he smelled.

"Oh, yes. He seems frailer than when I last saw him, but otherwise, he's fine. Listen, I'm sorry about last night. I wasn't expecting anyone to be up, and you startled me."

"Apology accepted. Is that what you wanted to talk to me about?"

"Oh, no, no, no," she stammered. *Why does this man make me so nervous?*

"My grandpa mentioned to me during a conversation we had yesterday that you have a good relationship with the police department. I was wondering if you could find out where this FedEx envelope came from and, if possible, who sent it. There's nothing on the outside showing it. I can't tell you why I need it, but it's vital that I find out."

"That shouldn't be too hard to do. I'll work on it myself, and if I need the police to help, I can certainly get it. I'm fairly good at this type of stuff," he said with a gentle smile. *Dear God, this is a beautiful woman. It's sad that she's been through so much pain.*

"May I ask you a question?" He was again wearing his shoulder holster.

"Go right ahead."

"Why do you carry a gun?"

"I'm a creature of habit, and you never know when you might need one. Does it bother you?"

"No, not really. I guess it just seems strange to me, given how safe it is around here. I guess I better get going now. I want to go check on my cousin at the hospital."

"I hope she makes it. I'll work on the FedEx mystery, and if I hear anything about the investigation into the cause of the accident, I'll let Ben know."

"Thanks, Russ. I really appreciate it."

She left and headed back to the house to get ready. Ben was still sitting on the porch, finishing his coffee while he waited for her. "I see you've met Russell. What do you think of him?"

"He seems nice but a little mysterious."

"He's a good fella. He's been through some hard times. Does a great job around here, though. I'm glad I have him. I'm ready to go to the hospital whenever you are."

"Ben, don't forget to take your pills before you leave," Ruth said, calling out from the doorway.

. . .

When they got to the hospital, there was no change in Melanie's condition. They were working to get her vital signs stabilized. Regina was still there, keeping a vigil watch. She looked so exhausted. Katherine's heart went out to her. She went to the bedside as she had done yesterday and held Melanie's hand, talking to her. She told her all about Sophie and what they had been doing together. She talked about anything to keep letting Melanie hear her voice. She had already been there for several hours and still wanted to see Chris. As she was standing to prepare to leave, Suzanne and Robert were entering the room.

Suzanne raced over to Melanie's bed, instantly crying hysterically, "Oh, dear God, my poor, sweet Melanie."

Regina was on the other side of the bed. "Just look at what your son has done to her! He's a monster. You don't belong here. I want you both to go."

They were both frozen, looking at her in disbelief.

She was yelling now. "Leave..... both of you!"

After they left the room, Dan went to Regina. "Sweet-heart, you are overwrought. I think you need to go home and get some rest."

"I'm *not* leaving my baby girl."

Katherine was touched. She had never witnessed her aunt Regina show so much emotion toward Melanie. Now more than ever, she wanted to talk to Chris.

Chapter Twenty-Eight

Katherine dropped Ben off at the house. She encouraged him to go get some rest. She borrowed his car and drove to the jail where they were holding Chris.

They escorted her into an area with a long wall that was divided into several booths with phones, enabling visitors to talk with prisoners through a glass partition. Someone brought Chris in and instructed him where to sit. He looked at Katherine with a blank expression. Katherine reached for her phone. Chris looked down, not reaching for his. She used her fist to bang on the glass, causing him to look up. He finally reached for his phone after seeing her point to the wall and put it to his ear.

"Chris, you have to tell me what happened."

"Is she alive?"

"Yes, she is alive, but I know there is no way you hurt her. I don't understand why you're saying that. I saw your house, Chris, and the pictures. You need to tell me the details."

He told her about getting the pictures, dropping Sophie off at Ben's, and the hideous argument.

"I told her I wanted her to just disappear, so she left. At

that point, all I wanted was to be rid of her. I think I blacked out after that. That's all I remember until the police showed up at the house."

"None of this makes sense, Chris. If that's what happened, why did you tell the police you tried to kill her?"

"I don't remember exactly what I told them, but I think I am responsible. Melanie had been complaining about for a couple of weeks before she left. Her car was acting funny, and the brakes were making a squealing noise. I told her I'd have it checked out while she was gone, but I forgot. Whatever was going on with her car is probably why she had the accident."

"Have you told your lawyer all of this?"

"I haven't spoken to anyone since they brought me in here. You're the first one I've told."

Katherine was absolutely beside herself. Chris was in jail for attempted murder, and he had nothing to do with it, as she had known all along. She needed to fix this and fix it fast before things spiraled out of control.

"Okay, Chris, this is what's going to happen. I'm going to go hire you a lawyer and Chris, when you see him you better tell him everything you've just told me. We have to get you out of here. Melanie needs you, and so does Sophie."

It was getting late in the afternoon. She needed to get to a computer to find a criminal attorney in the area. Driving back home, she couldn't get over what a mess everything was. She suddenly felt overwhelmed with the responsibility of so many others. Stewart's Addy was hanging on by a thread, Melanie might not make it, Chris had confessed to a crime he didn't commit, and she worried intensely about Ben looking so frail. She felt that maybe he should go in and see his doctor again soon. She made a mental note to take care of that too soon.

When she pulled the car around the back of the house, she

could see Ben and Russ talking over by the horse stable. He waved her over when he saw her get out of the car.

"What's going on, Grandpa? Is there any news about Melanie?"

"No, Katie. As far as I know, Melanie's condition has not changed. Russell has some news for us he got from the police. Tell her, Russell."

"I ran into a buddy of mine today who's been investigating the case. He said they have gone over what's left of Melanie's car with a fine-tooth comb. He said it appears the brakes failed, but more importantly, they may have been tampered with. That would make this an attempted homicide."

"I went to see Chris today. Melanie left the house alone after they argued. He couldn't have had anything to do with it."

"Yes, but from what I understand, she had been away. He could have tampered with them while she was gone and other than his word, how do you know for sure she left alone?" Russ retorted.

Katherine was fuming now. What business did this guy think he had to make judgments and jump to conclusions about her family, whom he barely knew?

"What are you now, some kind of authority on law enforcement? Leave the investigation to the ones that know what they are doing, not some ranch hand. Why don't you just go back to your horses?" She stormed away from him and went back toward the house.

"I'm sorry if she offended you, Russell. Katie has a lot on her mind, and she doesn't know about you."

"No offense taken, sir."

. . .

Katherine knew she had been cruel to him, but this guy just had a way of splitting her nerves. Ruth was right. He seemed a little too sure of himself, and she didn't trust him. She also remembered Ben mentioning that he had gone through some hard times. She wondered what he had gotten himself into and what kind of secret he was hiding from his past.

Ruth was cooking dinner when she got into the house. It smelled so good, and Katherine was starving, having not eaten anything the entire day. She wasn't paying attention because she was so worked up from her confrontation with Russ and almost tripped on the rug in front of the stairs again. She passed by the dining room on her way into the kitchen to see if she could be of any help. There, she noticed four places set. She knew Suzanne and Robert had picked up Sophie to take back to Melanie and Chris's house to stay– after they had gone over and cleaned up, of course– so why four place settings? When she went into the kitchen, she offered to help Ruth finish getting dinner ready. All that needed to be done was to put together a salad. While they were working, she asked Ruth why there were four places set.

"Ben invited that Russell for dinner. He usually does that at least once a week. I don't argue with him anymore about it because I know it won't do any good."

"Oh, great," Katherine said sarcastically, "I just had a run-in with him. This is not going to be pleasant. Ruth, I think we should move that rug in front of the stairs. I'm afraid it might cause Grandpa to fall."

Ruth turned and snapped at her. "Don't touch that rug. It was my mama's."

Her demeanor startled Katherine. "Well, maybe we could at least put some grippers under it to keep it in place."

Ruth regained her composure. "I suppose that might be a good idea. I'll take care of it."

Ben and Russ came in about an hour later. Russ looked at Katherine with a sarcastic smile. Clearly, he was sending her a message that his importance here was larger than she had thought. Regardless of what she was going through or had been through, he didn't like being treated with such disrespect. She looked back at him with an ill-humored expression. For Ben's sake, she tried to be cordial throughout dinner, making light, unimportant conversation.

"So, Russ, how's Lucky doing?"

"He's doing great and is a remarkable horse. He's a funny little guy, too. He tries to dig into my pockets, looking for a treat every time I go near him."

Katherine couldn't help but laugh. "That sounds like Lucky." She felt a pang of jealousy that this man had a relationship with her horse.

Russ stood then, holding his glass. "I'm going to go get more tea. Can I get anyone else anything?"

Good grief.... he is acting as if he thinks he's part of the family, Katherine thought.

They all said they were fine but thanked him. He went to the counter and poured his tea. He saw Ben's pocket watch lying beside the bowl containing some lemon slices. He picked it up and flipped it open. With his all-knowing smile, he was not surprised that the picture inside was of Elizabeth, not Ruth. He didn't think she was the woman Ben thought she was and felt she had the wool completely pulled over his eyes. He didn't trust her any further than he could throw her.

196

After they had just about finished eating the delicious tilapia Ruth had prepared, she stood up, taking a couple of plates with her. "I made us a fresh blueberry pie for dessert. I'll just get it and bring it back in here."

"I can't believe you're actually going to let me have dessert, Ruthie," said Ben.

"Don't fool yourself, Ben. I made it with all fat-free ingredients. Things don't have to be unhealthy, and you need to watch what you eat."

"Everything was delicious, Ruth. Thank you," Russ said politely after dessert. He helped clear the table and said good-night to everyone.

When Ruth and Katherine finished cleaning up, it was only eight, but Katherine was exhausted. All she wanted to do was go upstairs, take a hot shower, and curl up in bed, but she still needed to find an attorney for Chris.

"Grandpa, would you mind terribly if I used your laptop for a few minutes? My notebook needs to be charged, and I want to see if I can find a good criminal attorney for Chris."

"Not at all, Katie. You go help yourself."

She headed down the hall toward his study. Finding one shouldn't be too tricky, especially if she checked out reviews about them online. When she went to sit down in the chair behind his desk, she hit her knee on a file drawer that was partially ajar. It hadn't closed properly because a file folder was sticking partially up. When she went to push it back down properly, she noticed it was the folder her grandpa kept regarding the property and his estate. She wondered why he would have pulled that out and became concerned. She worriedly concluded that he felt his health was deteriorating and wanted to make sure things were in order. He had always been into details, so this didn't surprise her, but it did make her want to get him to his doctor as soon as possible. Once she finished her research, she jotted down the name and phone number of the attorney. She intended to call him in the morning to retain him for Chris. Once she finally made it upstairs, she skipped the hot shower, changed her clothes, and went straight to bed. She had nightmares about being chased by a mysterious stranger.

She woke up the next morning feeling as though she had a hangover, even though she had had nothing to drink the night before. She was sure it was from all the stress from the past several days and from not having a very restful sleep. Running all night in her dreams had seemed so real, she felt like she had done it. Her head was splitting. She took some Tylenol, got a hot shower, dressed, and headed downstairs. Today would be another busy day.

She could hear Ben and Ruth talking in the kitchen when she descended the stairs.

"Where did you see it last?" she was saying.

"I can't really recall. I know I had it on me last night, but now I can't find it for the life of me."

"Good morning, everyone," Katherine said. "What are you guys talking about? Is something lost?"

"Ben can't find his pocket watch."

All three of them worked on it together. Ben didn't go anywhere without his pocket watch. He cherished it. They did everything they could and looked everywhere he had been the day and night before. It just wasn't to be found. Katherine looked at Ruth, who gave her a knowing look. Another item was missing, and Russ just so happened to have been in the house the night before. Exactly who was this man that had totally gained her grandfather's trust?

As she was leaving the room, she heard Ruth say to him, "We'll look for it again later, but for now, you need to go take your pills. You look a bit pale today."

Chapter Twenty-Nine

Katherine wished she could have done more to help him continue to look, but she had to get her day started. She went back up to her bedroom with her coffee and contacted the attorney on Chris's behalf. She paid his retainer over the phone, and he assured her he would go to the jail that morning and get Chris's side of the story. Having been a former DA, he also had a good working relationship with the DA's office. He said that unless they had some hard evidence, the case against Chris would probably be changed to a lesser charge or dropped completely. She breathed a sigh of relief and then called Chris's mother to give her the information as well. The next call she made was to Ben's doctor. She had always called him Dr. Bob growing up. He'd been their family physician for years. She was able to get an appointment for the next morning. She'd take him herself.

She didn't want to bother Ben, feeling that perhaps he needed to stay home that day. There was nothing he could do, just sitting around the hospital, so she asked him if she could borrow his car.

Ruth spoke up, saying, "You know what, I'll drive you in my car, Katherine. I'd like to see Melanie for myself."

"Well, thank you, Ruth. I know Uncle Dan and Aunt Regina would appreciate your concern."

"Just give me ten minutes, and we'll be on our way."

During the drive to the hospital, Katherine brought up the missing pocket watch. "Ruth, do you think Russ may have taken it? It seems awfully coincidental that it disappeared the morning after he had been in the house the night before."

"I don't want to think that, but it might be true. I can't believe he'd take anything that belongs to Ben. He seems to have a lot of admiration and respect for him. Oh, dag nab bit."

"What's wrong, Ruth?"

"I think we might have a flat tire," she said, pulling over to the side of the road. They weren't on a busy highway. Ruth had taken one of the back ways to avoid traffic, so it wasn't likely anyone would stop to help.

"Should I call AAA?" Katherine asked her.

Ruth swung her head around, looking at Katherine as though she had suddenly grown two extra heads. "AAA????? It's only a flat tire. Damn, girl, don't you know nothing about cars?"

By then, they were both out of the car and heading back to the trunk. "Well, no, not really. I've never had an interest in learning and didn't really need to."

"Well, you should. My daddy owned a garage when I was growing up. He fixed up an old car and gave it to me when I turned sixteen, but before he gave me the keys, he said, *Ruth, if you're going to own a car, you need to make sure you know some basic things.* He made me learn how to change a tire, change my wiper blades, and check my fluids, among other things. It's come in mighty handy over the years. I'm sure glad he did."

Once Ruth finished changing the tire, they got back on their way. Regina and Dan were in Melanie's room when they arrived. Ruth went to both, offering her sympathy for what had happened to their daughter. Regina looked ragged. She had not left Melanie's side the entire time she had been in the hospital, sleeping in the recliner next to her bed and taking a shower in the adjacent bathroom. Dan brought her some clothes to change into. Melanie's coloring was looking better, and the nurse said her vital signs were stabilizing when she came in to take them. They took them every half hour. Katherine had her phone silenced but noticed Mildred was calling her. She took her phone out into the hallway to answer it.

"Hi, Mildred. Is everything okay?"

"I'm sorry to say I'm calling with sad news, Katherine. Abby passed away just a little while ago."

"Oh, Mildred, I wish I could be there. How's Stewart?"

"Believe it or not, he's doing well, considering. I think he might be feeling some sort of relief. It's so hard to watch someone you love suffer. No one wants to experience that."

"I'll call him once we hang up."

"I'm sure that would mean a lot to him. He really is a very kind man, Katherine. While I've got you, I wanted to tell you how lovely your home is. You've decorated it in a way that feels quite inviting."

"Thank you, Mildred. I wanted it to feel that way. Thank you so very much for being there for Stewart. You have gone over and above the call of duty."

"It has been my pleasure. I know how it feels to lose the love of your life. We all need someone to lean on sometimes. I'll probably head back in a few days once I know he's going to be okay."

After she hung up with Mildred, she called Stewart. "Hi, Stewart. Mildred just called me and told me the news. I'm so sorry. I wish I could be there for you."

"I understand, Katherine. You are where you belong right now. Mildred has been very kind and a great comfort. If it's alright with you, after she leaves, I'd like to take care of Muffin. I love that little guy. How's your cousin?"

"She's getting a little better, I think. She's still in a coma, but her vital signs are beginning to stabilize. I just wish she'd wake up. I hate seeing her like this. Thank you for offering to take care of Muffin. I know how much he loves you."

"I think animals can sense people and know the ones that like them."

"I totally agree with you. Stewart, please call me if you need anything or just need someone to talk to. You're like family to me."

After they hung up, she went over and sat in a small sitting area that was close by. She had so much admiration for Stewart and Mildred as well. They had both lost the love of their lives, just as she had, but handled it so much better. She felt so grateful for their wisdom. They were both good examples and had shown her that life could go on after a tremendous loss. She felt she was finally on her way to making that happen for herself; at least, she hoped so.

Ruth drove her back home later that afternoon. When they were pulling up the driveway, Katherine spotted Russ crouched down in front of the rose bushes along the side of the house, hacking away at them with hedge clippers.

When they got closer, Katherine said, "Ruth, let me out here, please."

Walking quickly, she stomped up to Russ. "What are you doing?" she said angrily.

"Ben said the rose bushes looked overgrown and asked me to prune them."

"This is *not* how to prune roses. You are going to ruin them. They are a very delicate flower. Give me those," she said huffily, reaching for the clippers. "I'll take care of it."

"Why don't you just do that, Miss Fix-it." Russ left her standing there, glaring at him.

Ben was sitting on the porch around the corner. Hearing the exchange, he couldn't help but chuckle silently.

Russ walked over to the steps leading up to the porch and leaned against one of the columns. "That didn't go so well."

"Katie tends to speak her mind, Russell; always has."

Ruth didn't speak to Russ when she walked up to the porch after getting out of her car but went over to Ben and kissed the top of his head. "You been taking care of yourself today?"

"Yes, Ruthie, I have. I haven't left the house all day, but I'm going out in a few minutes to the barbershop, with your permission, of course." He said, chuckling.

"I'm going in. Let me know if you need anything."

Katherine walked up to the porch a few minutes later after salvaging the damage Russ had done to the roses. She merely glanced at Russ but went over to Ben and kissed his cheek before settling into the other rocker. "Hi, Grandpa."

"My sweet Katie, I was just telling Russell that I thought you'd be willing to ride Lucky this afternoon so he could stretch his legs. He gets stiff without enough exercise and Russell doesn't have time to finish up all of them. He's got some special plans for tonight."

"I'd be happy to, Grandpa. I haven't even had time to say hello to Lucky yet. Russ, just give me a few minutes to freshen up. I'll meet you at the stables."

Katherine went inside and then upstairs to find her riding boots in her closet. She hadn't bothered ever taking them because this was the only place she ever rode horses. She stopped by the kitchen to grab a water bottle out of the refrigerator on her way. By the time she got to the stables, Russ had the horses ready. When Lucky saw her, he gently walked away from Russ and directly toward her. When he got to her, he nuzzled her cheek.

Katherine grinned as she reached up, stroking the sides of his long head. "Hey there, fella. I've really missed you." Lucky nickered at her softly. Russ stood back and watched this extreme display of affection between horse and human in amazement. Few people had that special touch with horses that made them happy, but Katherine certainly had the gift. This horse loved her and had missed her as well. He put his long nose down by her hands, appearing to give her gentle kisses, which made Katherine toss back her head in a deep, throaty, joyous laughter, "There are no treats in there, you silly goose, but thanks for the kisses." Russ was certain he had never seen a more beautiful woman in his life than he was seeing at this very moment. Her long, auburn, curly hair was pulled up in a ponytail on the back of her head, but the humidity of the day had loosened sprigs that were gently falling along the cheeks of her olive skin. Her smile lit up the stable as if a light had just been turned on.

She turned to see Russ watching them. His expression was one of esteemed admiration. Despite the scar on his face, he was such a handsome man. Under different circumstances, they could have been friends. That was not possible, though– he was too quiet and mysterious, and then there was the suspicion that he had been stealing things.

"I'm sorry to have kept you so long." She looked back at

Lucky, holding his rein with one hand and stroking him with the other. "Isn't he majestic, Russ?"

"You haven't kept me long at all, and yes, he is majestic. This scene between the two of you is quite beautiful. It's rare for humans to have such a deep connection with their horses. He is yours, isn't he?"

"Yes. My grandpa gave him to me when I turned sixteen. He taught me how to take care of him. He was just a little guy then. I think we had love at first sight, both being youngsters," she said, chuckling. "I know you have plans, so I guess we should be on our way." Something about the way he was looking at her had made her somewhat uncomfortable.

They started just walking the horses. Russ said, "I wanted to let you know in private that I found out who sent the FedEx envelope to your cousin's address. The sender's name was Theresa Hollingsworth from Boston."

Katherine looked at him, confused. "I don't know anyone by that name in Boston or why they would send pictures of my cousin to her husband. To my knowledge, they don't know anyone there. I need to find out if what this person did was illegal. How were you able to get the information?"

"I have a set of special skills from my former employment. It comes in handy sometimes. Also, sometimes it's in who you know? As far as the legality, the person who did this could have committed an illegal act if your cousin did not know the pictures were being taken and/or if they inflicted any harm in doing so."

"You seem to have a fair amount of knowledge about this stuff." She noticed he was again wearing his arm holster with the pistol. "Is it because of your former employer that you carry a gun?"

"Something like that."

"Did you get injured doing that job? Is that how you got your scar?"

His jaw tensed up. "No" was all he said.

It was such a beautiful afternoon. The sun was high in the sky, and a gentle breeze had started to blow. The tall grass was swinging in the wind. Riding Lucky was giving Katherine more joy than she had experienced in quite some time. She could sense that he was happy as well. She truly loved her horse. She thought about asking Russ about Ben's pocket watch but was enjoying herself so much and their conversation without tension that she decided to wait for another time. When they were headed back toward the stable, Katherine took off with Lucky on a fast run, laughing the entire time. She felt as free as the wind.

When she put Lucky back in his stall, he rested his head on top of hers. "Thanks for the hug, buddy. I love you." She looked over toward Russ. He had already taken Blackie, Ben's horse, free of his reins, but he was still following him. Truly, that was a sign he trusted him. After he put him in his stall, as Russ was reaching in and rubbing his neck, he let out a powerful breath in his face. Russ laughed. Horses only did that when they were showing affection, respect, and accepting a human as part of the family. Regardless of how Blackie felt about Russ, Katherine could never accept him as part of the family.

Chapter Thirty

It was early in the evening. After dinner, Katherine decided she would go out on the porch and relax a bit. So much had happened that day. It was hard to comprehend it all. Poor Stewart had lost Abby, but in a way, it was a blessing. At least she would no longer suffer, but just as importantly, Stewart would not have to suffer anymore, either. She was glad she had been able to find an attorney for Chris. Hopefully, the investigation would be over soon, and the charges would be dismissed. The attorney had mentioned to her that he should be able to get Chris out on bail, although the challenge with that was going to be that he had confessed. She hadn't heard from anyone today, so she did not know if that had happened yet or not. Melanie's coloring looked a little better today. She wished she could say the same about her aunt Regina. She was going to make herself sick if she didn't take care of herself. Thinking about that reminded her about the doctor's appointment she had made for Ben in the morning. He was probably long overdue for a checkup, although if he were overdue for a checkup, Ruth would have made sure he had one. She doted over him like a mama bear over her cubs.

.   .   .

Then, there was the mystery surrounding Russ. Her feelings about him and her opinion of him were so complex. One minute she totally hated him; the next, she didn't trust him and then could enjoy him as she had this afternoon. He could, with just a look, completely unnerve her. He could be quite sarcastic when he wanted to be. If he was such a bad person, why did Ben think so much of him? He was usually such an excellent judge of character. To her knowledge, no one had pulled the wool over his eyes in her entire life. Then there was the whole weapon thing. He seemed to never be without it. Why would anyone be so suspicious of others that they would feel the need to carry a weapon 24/7? She felt there was more to him than met the eye and that he might be hiding something or hiding out.

She heard a car pulling up the driveway, going past the side of the porch to park in front of the garages where the other cars were parked. A beautiful woman got out. She didn't recognize her. She had long jet-black hair and was wearing a casual outfit of capris and a tank top with sandals. She couldn't get a good look at her face because of the angle. She took off running toward the stairs leading to the apartment over the garage, squealing as she saw Russ approaching her. He had an enormous grin on his face, showing his perfect white smile with his arms open wide. She jumped in them when they reached each other. He held her tightly as he spun her around. She was much shorter than he was, so it lifted her feet from the ground. When he put her down, they walked arm-in-arm toward the stairs.

.   .   .

The scene bothered her for some reason that she couldn't figure out. She had to admit that she had a physical attraction to him, but she could never get involved with him emotionally. She had gotten the same feeling from him. Russ didn't seem like the kind of man that would be in a relationship, but clearly, there was a strong bond between him and this woman. She pushed him from her thoughts and went to take a hot shower and relax alone in her room. Ruth had put fresh towels on her bed. She was so thoughtful. She removed her locket and went into the bathroom. To take away her stresses from the day before going to bed, she filled the soaking tub with some bath salts instead of taking a shower.

When she got up the next morning, the first thing she did was call to check on Melanie's condition. Her aunt Regina told her she thought her condition was improving, although she still had not woken up. She also told her that the police Investigator had stopped by late afternoon the day before. He said that there were indications that the brakes on Melanie's car had been tampered with. They were waiting for the results from taking fingerprints. That put a new spin on things, making it premeditated. She would go see her after she took her grandpa to his doctor's appointment. She had not mentioned it to Ruth because she did not want to cause her to worry about him.

She went to the exam with him. The Nurse did the normal preliminary work. She furrowed her brow when she took his blood pressure. Dr. Bob came in shortly thereafter. He was in a no-nonsense mood. Normally, he would come in acting like his jolly old self, but today he was all business.

"Ben, it's good to see you. Tell me how you've been feeling."

"A little tired at times, and sometimes I wake up sweating

at night, but otherwise, the same." The night sweats were a surprise to Katherine.

"Any shortness of breath or chest pains?"

"Only sometimes. Not too often."

"How about your eating habits? Are you practicing the healthy eating we talked about before?"

Ben chuckled at that question. "Oh, you bet I am. Ruthie won't let me put anything in my mouth that she hasn't either made herself or approved of."

"That's good to hear."

"Why all the questions, Bob?"

"Ben, your blood pressure is sky high and so is your heart rate. I have a good mind to put you in the hospital to get it under control. I'm going to order some blood work and put a rush on the results. I'll decide on your treatment when the results come back later today. For now, though, I'm going to add another medication to your regimen. I want you to take them as soon as you get them. Katherine, please make sure you pick up this prescription on your way home. I will have it sent over and ready for you at the pharmacy we have on record."

"I absolutely will, Dr. Bob. Is there cause for alarm?" She was enormously worried.

"We'll know more when I get the blood work results. I'll call you this afternoon. Please leave your cell number with my nurse."

When they left the office, she was inwardly shaken. She had been worried about her grandpa ever since she had arrived. What if something happened to him? She couldn't bear the thought of it. She called her aunt Regina and told her something important had come up and that she would not be at the hospital until later, but she was thinking to herself that she might not be able to go at all. She had spent many days and nights beside Melanie's bedside and would sometimes just hold her hand. Other times, she would talk about funny stories about when they were younger growing up and even some about the years the two couples had spent together. It was odd, but she didn't get sad mentioning Jason's name. The memories she was talking about with Melanie were very happy ones that she would cherish forever.

Ruth's car wasn't in the driveway when they got home. She gave Ben his medicine and made him something healthy to eat. After lunch, she got him settled in his bed to rest. She put his cell phone on the nightstand next to him so he could let her know if he needed anything. She put her number on speed dial for him, so all he had to do was just push a button.

She took a book out on the porch to sit and read but couldn't really concentrate. The guest Russ had the night before appeared to be gone.

Unable to concentrate, she went up to take a relaxing shower and possibly lay down herself. She took off her locket, as always, and picked out some summer sweats to slip into after her shower. When drying off, someone walked past the bathroom door. She called out, but no one answered. Probably just her imagination or her extreme fatigue. She towel-dried her wet hair and went back into her bedroom, walking over to the dresser where she had put her locket when she took it off. But it wasn't there. She looked all over the top and then on the floor in front, assuming it had just slipped off. It was nowhere to be found. She scanned her entire bedroom, especially the area all around the dresser, but came up empty. Hearing the screen door slamming downstairs caused her to go look out of her bedroom window. Russ was walking away from the house toward the garage. He was carrying his tool pouch. She flew down the stairs out the door, chasing after him, calling his name. He stopped and looked back at her. When she got to him, she was fuming.

"Give me back my locket, you common thief!"

"I do not know what you're talking about, Katherine. What locket?"

"You know what locket. It was in my room a few minutes ago on my dresser, and now it's gone. Now, give it back." she was yelling now.

"I have not been in the house at all, and why would you think I'd steal your locket?"

"It's gone, and you're the only one here besides me and my grandpa."

He took hold of her upper arm and looked her directly in the eye. Despite her anger, she felt herself melting. "It wasn't me. Why don't you go ask Ruth?"

"Ruth is not even here," she said, motioning toward her empty parking space.

"That's funny. I saw her walking away from the house about 10 minutes ago when I was repairing a piece of lattice on the side of the porch. Now, leave me alone, Katherine. I'm not your guy." He stalked away from her.

She had never hated anyone as much as she hated this man at this very moment. He was lying, but she couldn't imagine why he would try to blame Ruth. She would have to figure all of this out later. She needed to go check on Ben.

As she was walking back toward the house, Ruth was driving up the lane. She parked her car and walked around to the trunk.

Katherine turned and walked toward her. "Do you need help with your bags, Ruth?"

"I just have one but thank you for offering." She tilted her head, looking at Katherine, puzzled.

"Are you feeling all right? You look a little pale." Katherine considered telling Ruth why but decided against it. Ruth already disliked Russ, and this would put the icing on the cake.

"I'm fine. Just tired, I guess. I've had a lot on my mind lately."

"Indeed, you have. Why don't you go lay down and rest?"

"I think I'd rather go ride Lucky. He has a way of relaxing me."

Ruth opened the trunk of her car after Katherine walked away and retrieved a burlap sack.

When Katherine went up to change into her riding outfit, she stopped to check on Ben. He seemed to be resting well. She decided she'd wait until Dr. Bob called with the test results to tell Ruth. There was no need to worry her until she could tell her everything all at once.

She had been riding for about an hour and decided to find a way to go search Russ's apartment when he wasn't around to try to find her locket. She was looking forward to getting away from him once everything was resolved and she could go home. Her cell rang when she was nearing the barn. She brought Lucky to a stop so she could answer it.

"Hello."

"Katherine, it's Bob Evans. I have Ben's test results. His LDL level is dangerously high, and most of his other results are not within a good range, either. I'm going to entirely change the medications he's taking, and I'd like to see him again in a week. I'd also like for you to pick up a blood pressure kit so you can monitor his blood pressure. I want you to take it three times a day and call the readings into my nurse."

"Of course. I'll take care of that right away."

"I knew I could count on you, Katherine. That's the only reason I'm not putting him in the hospital." He paused. "Yet."

After they ended the call, she headed faster toward the

stable. She dismounted outside the door, and when she was walking Lucky to his area; she spotted Russ at the other end grooming Blackie. He was talking to him as he worked, as though he was talking to a real person. Blackie was obviously enjoying the conversation because he started nuzzling his nose and cheek. It made Russ laugh. He looked so likable at that moment. She wished things could be different between them.

She was placing Lucky's harness and the reins on the hook just outside his stall. Suddenly, Lucky became very agitated. He was jumping up, lifting his front legs into the air, and rocking his head violently.

"Calm down, boy. What's gotten into you?" She was reaching in to rub his neck when she heard it. There was no mistaking what it was. The loud rattle was just behind her. She turned, screaming, and lost her balance, hitting her head against the wooden post as she fell, facing the direction Russ was standing. He moved as fast as a cheetah, taking a very deliberate stance and grabbing his gun at the same time. With one very accurate shot, he blew the rattlesnake's head off.

Katherine was sobbing and shaking. He ran to her side, falling to his knees and wrapping his arms around her, clasping her tightly. "Are you all right?"

She could barely speak more than a whisper. "Yes." She was still sobbing and had turned her head into his chest.

He didn't attempt to let go. He turned his head at an angle and rested it on top of her head. He was entranced by how good she smelled. It was like walking through a field of honeysuckle on a beautiful late spring day. He wished he didn't dislike this woman so much, but then, he had been cautious not to get involved with any woman since...

She eventually regained her composure and pulled away from him. "I'm sorry. I don't usually act like that."

"You're more than welcome. I think most people would have reacted exactly as you did."

She looked up at him with a perplexed look before standing up and brushing herself off. This man, whom she normally hated to the depths of her soul, had made her feel totally safe. While heading back up to the house, she couldn't help but wonder, *Who exactly are you, Russell Woodson?*

Chapter Thirty-One

When she went upstairs to change, she was still feeling quite shaken, but she decided to go pick up what she needed for Ben at the drugstore. Then, she would sit down with Ruth and let her know what was going on. When she got back, Ruth was sitting on the porch.

"Ruth, I need to talk to you, but there's something I have to take care of first. Will you wait here for me?"

"Of course I will. You haven't seemed yourself the past couple of days. I'll wait right here for me, and we'll talk as long as you like."

This would not be easy. Katherine could tell that Ruth dearly loved Ben just by the way she took such good care of him if nothing else. He was sitting in his chair in the parlor when she went in.

"Hi, Grandpa. You're looking much better. Dr. Bob called and said he'd like to change your medications to get some of your levels under control, and he wants your blood pressure to be taken several times a day and have the results called into his office. He wants to see you again in a week."

"I'm feeling much better after that long rest, Katie. I'm

sure everything will be just fine, and I'll do exactly what Bob wants me to do."

Katherine kissed his cheek, gave him his new medications, and returned to the porch to talk to Ruth.

She sat down in the rocker next to her.

"Ruth, what I wanted to talk to you about is Grandpa. I've noticed his health seems to be declining, so I made an appointment with his doctor and took him in this morning." Ruth frowned at her. "I know I should have told you, but I didn't want to worry you. I'm sorry. Anyway, they did extensive blood work, and none of it came back the way it should, especially his LDL level, and his blood pressure was very high. The doctor put him on a new medication regimen and wants to see him in a week. He also wants me to take his blood pressure several times a day and call the readings into his office."

Ruth looked angry. "You should have let me handle this, Katherine. I know he's your grandpa, but he's my husband. I'm the one who should take care of him. Show me the new medications, and I will see that he takes them, and I will take charge of his blood pressure. Is that clear?"

"Yes, Ruth, it is. All I ask is that you let me know what his readings are when you take them."

"I will do that. I'm going to check on him and start dinner."

Katherine stayed where she was. She didn't quite understand Ruth's reaction. She knew she would be upset, but the anger toward her had surprised her. She didn't even thank her for her concern. Maybe once she got to know Ruth a little better, she would be able to understand why she reacted the way she did. Spotting Russ over by the garage, she decided to go over and talk to him. He turned toward her when he saw her approaching.

"I wanted to thank you for what you did earlier. It was one time I was glad you had your pistol with you. Where did you learn to shoot like that? You were deadly accurate."

He thought about making something up, but for some reason, he couldn't explain; he wanted her to know the truth. He sat down on a large boulder next to the garage. "I haven't shared this with many people other than those who knew about it and, of course, my little sister, who you saw the other day when she arrived."

"Wait, that was your sister? I thought she was your girlfriend."

He smiled at her as he continued. "There is not a woman in my life, at least not anymore." His jaw tightened, and he looked down at a stick he had picked up from the ground. He suddenly had a despondent expression on his face. He looked away from her at the rolling hills of the pasture as he continued. "The former employment I mentioned to you before was the Secret Service. I was an investigative Special Agent. I was also married at the time. Seven years ago, we were returning from going out to dinner. A truck ran a stoplight and rammed right into us. I was injured. My wife was killed, along with the baby she was carrying." He paused; the pain on his face was difficult to look at. "My scar is from that accident. The injury affected the hearing in my left ear to the extent that I no longer qualified for the Agency, which requires perfect hearing. When I returned to the area, Ben offered me a job taking care of the ranch. He knows my father well, so he became aware of my situation. Working for him has been a godsend. He treats me like a son, and the work I do for him has been therapeutic. There is nothing I wouldn't do for Ben; I want you to know that."

Katherine was speechless. "Oh, Russ, I'm so very sorry. I know what it feels like to lose someone. You lost your wife and your child at the same time. What a burden that must have been."

"It still is. It's the reason I don't have a relationship with anyone. I never want to experience that kind of pain again. I'd rather spend my life alone."

"But are you happy, Russ? I mean, *really* happy with your life as it is now?"

"I'm happy enough. Life is what it is sometimes."

"Maybe you could try to recapture some of the things that used to be a part of your life that made you happy."

"I'm not sure I know how to do that, Katherine." He stood up then, looking rather somber.

"Well, I better get back to work. I have a couple of things to finish before it gets dark."

* * *

As Katherine returned to the house, her thoughts about Russ and his situation consumed her. He had suffered a significant loss, just as she had. He was living a shell of a life, just like she had. Her opinion of him had suddenly changed. She had misjudged him. He had a kind soul. She now understood his abrupt mood swings. He was protecting himself from having any close relationship with anyone, man or woman. He had become a loner and intended to keep it that way. She no longer feared him or lacked trust in him.

* * *

The next day, Regina was once again at Melanie's bedside. She had barely left her side since the accident three weeks ago. This morning did not differ from the rest. She was holding Melanie's hand with her head resting on the side of the bed.

She suddenly felt Melanie's fingers start to move in her hand. "Mama, is that you?"

Regina pressed the call button. "*Nurse, Nurse, she's awake!*" A whole host of staff members came rushing in and began tending to Melanie. Regina stood back with her hand on her heart, looking on, overwhelmed with emotion.

After a few minutes, one nurse said to Regina, "You can come to see your daughter now."

Regina walked to Melanie's bedside, leaning over, trying to wrap her arms around her without hurting her. She was weeping. Her baby girl was finally awake. "Oh, Melanie, my sweet baby. You've come back to me. I was so frightened that I was going to lose you. I was afraid that I would never have the opportunity to tell you how very proud I am of you and the woman you are. You're so much more than I've ever been as a mother. I love you so much, Melanie. Can you ever forgive me?"

Her voice was weak, but Melanie managed to say, "I love you, Mama. There's nothing to forgive."

Regina was trying to regain her composure but was still overwhelmed by the feelings exploding deep within her. She gently ran her hand along Melanie's cheek. "One day soon, when you're fully recovered, I want to share with you the details of my childhood that made me who I've been. I won't ever be that person again. I want you and me to build a very special bond if you're willing."

"I'd like nothing better, Mama."

Regina called Katherine, letting her know Melanie was out of her coma. She got dressed so fast she didn't remember even doing it. She and Ben fled to the hospital.

When they got to Melanie's room, the atmosphere was joyful. Regina looked transformed, and Dan smiled. She went to Melanie's bedside and embraced her in a warm hug.

She pulled partially away, saying, "You don't know how glad I am to see you. I love you so much, Mel."

Melanie said sleepily, "Love you more."

A Nurse entered the room at that point. "I know ya'll are glad our girl is back with us, but she still needs her rest so she can regain her strength and continue to heal. Why don't you come back a while later?"

As they prepared to leave, Melanie said, "Kat, I need to talk to you alone for a minute."

Katherine walked over to her bedside and sat down in the chair. Regina and Dan respectfully left the room.

"We don't need to talk about anything that happened, Mel. I'm sorry I judged you, and I'm even more sorry for the things I said to you."

"I need to say this. I did nothing to dissuade Whitney's advances. I was enjoying the attention. When he returned that night to return the cooler, he stayed long after everyone else went to bed. He made my last drink. I think he put something in it, Kat. I wouldn't have cheated on Chris of my own free will for anything. There's nothing I can do to prove it, but I know in my heart that's what happened."

"You'll have to find a way to let this go, Mel, and stop blaming yourself. We all make mistakes in life, and hopefully, we learn from some of them. We can talk more about this or anything you want later, but for now, you need to take care of yourself. I love you more than you know."

"Love you more." With that, Melanie closed her eyes and fell into a peaceful sleep.

When Katherine was driving home with Ben, she felt like she was floating on air. Everything was coming together. It appeared Melanie was going to have a full recovery. Hopefully, with the new medications, Ben's health will improve. There was still the issue of getting the charges dropped against Chris. His parents had been conversing with the attorney daily, and even though it might take a little time, he felt it would happen. At least now, they knew why he had confessed to trying to kill Melanie. She recalled him saying that if only he had remembered having her car checked, none of this would have happened.

The atmosphere surrounding everyone had totally changed. It was as if the sun had been hiding behind the clouds and suddenly had decided to shine down on everyone.

When they got home, Ben put on his favorite fishing outfit and, on his way out of the house, stopped to speak to Russ, who was working on the porch's loose railing.

"Hi there, Russell. I'm going to head down to the beach to try to catch some fish. Would you care to join me?"

Russ smiled at him. He truly appreciated and admired this man. "Normally I would, Ben, but I need to finish this post. It's too loose to be safe."

"Well, if you finish up what you're working on, come down and join me. If I'm lucky enough to catch something, why don't you come for dinner?"

"I'd like that very much, sir. Thank you for the offer."

Ben walked off with a wave of his fishing hat.

Katherine stopped to speak to Russ as she was climbing the porch steps.

"Hi, Russ. How's everything going?" she said casually.

"Not bad, Katherine. Just trying to finish up some work I started."

"I was wondering. You wouldn't want to go for a horseback ride later?"

"Does that mean you don't want me to?"

She gave a small laugh. "I was actually asking if you'd be willing to."

He smiled back at her. "That would be nice. A good way to end the day. I'll let you know when I finish." He watched her walk into the house. Something about her had softened.

He couldn't help but think, *My God, that's a beautiful woman.*

There didn't appear to be anyone around when she got into the house. She was starving, having not eaten anything so far that day. She had flown out the door so quickly to see Melanie that she hadn't even had a cup of coffee, let alone breakfast. When she went into the kitchen, she noticed Ruth had all her grandpa's pills set out in an orderly fashion on the countertop. The blood pressure machine was sitting next to it with a pad of paper and a pen for recording his readings. She glanced at what they had been so far today, and they did not look all that bad. Ruth had even written the date and time they'd been taken. She seemed to have things totally under control, causing her to feel a great sigh of relief. She checked the refrigerator and pulled out some turkey, cheese, and lettuce to make a sandwich. She noticed that the cheese was made with whole milk. Ruth had obviously picked that up accidentally, which was very easy to do. She tossed it in the trash and would pick up a replacement non-fat the next time she went out. The mayonnaise was also high in fat. She tossed that, too.

What she needed to do most right now was sit and relax for a while. She had called Olivia to see if she knew anyone with the name that had sent the pictures. It had been Tess. She was obviously trying to make trouble for Melanie because she had wanted Whitney, but he wouldn't have anything to do with her. It would be up to Chris and Melanie to decide if they wanted to take out a civil suit on her. Knowing them the way she did, she doubted they would. They'd probably like just to put the whole thing behind them.

· · ·

She took her lunch into the parlor, curled up on the couch, and watched TV while she ate her sandwich. She realized once she got in there that she had forgotten to grab a water. Before going back into the kitchen, she raised a couple of windows. A cold front had come through and taken away the humidity. She loved feeling the fresh breeze flowing in. Russ was hard at work on the porch railing close to the window. She heard one of her favorite shows coming on and hurried back toward the parlor, not paying attention. She hit the rug in front of the steps and sent it flying, landing partially up against a wall. She went over to put it back in its place and noticed a loose board from the old hardwoods. She bent down to push it down more securely when she noticed something shining from underneath. She went to get the poker from the fireplace hearth and returned to the board. Getting down on her knees and using the poker, she pried it open more. She tossed the poker aside. When she saw what was resting on the subfloor underneath, she felt as if someone had punched her in the gut.

Chapter Thirty-Two

Reaching in, she pulled the items within the space and set them down on the step next to her as she pulled them out. Folded underneath all of it, securing everything in place, was the beloved quilt her grandmother had made for her. There were several pieces of her grandmother's silver, an expensive hand-blown glass vase, Ben's pocket watch, and her locket, among other things. She sat there just gazing at the items in total shock when she heard someone come up behind her.

"You just couldn't keep your nose to yourself. Could Ya?"

Katherine spun her head around, and there stood Ruth, not even two feet away from her, holding the poker that Katherine had just tossed aside. Not having yet been told that Melanie was out of her coma and would recover, she said, "That cousin of yours couldn't either, asking way too many questions, but I took care of her. She won't be talking to anybody."

"Ruth, I don't understand. What is all of this? Why were these things hidden under the board?"

Ruth laughed bewitchingly. "You really are as dumb as a rock, aren't ya? You see, Katherine, I've been after Ben for years. I grew up poor. Never had nothing. When Elizabeth died, I saw my chance. I married him for his money. Once he died, I'd have everything. Then I found his will and discovered that he was leaving you practically everything and very little to me. That sneaky cousin of yours caught me in his study, going through his files, and started to ask a lot of questions. I knew I had to get her out of the picture. I punched a hole in the brake fluid, just big enough for it to drip out so she wouldn't have any when she eventually went to put her foot on the brake, causing an accident. Turned out even better than I'd planned, too. That knowledge I have about cars paid off. Then there's that Russell. He's too much of a watcher. I've felt his eyes watching my every movement ever since I got here. It's as if he's seeing right through me, like telepathy or whatever you call it. I started to make things go missing so Ben would get rid of him for stealing, but he never believed Russell could do something like that and thought the things had just been misplaced."

"What about my locket? You weren't even here when I lost it."

"You didn't *think* I was here. I parked my car around the front of the house so it would look like I was gone. It just took me a couple of minutes to go up, grab it, and walk out with it. It was a thrill when I saw you accusing Russell. I could hear you all the way to my car. Then, I waited a bit before pulling back up the driveway. Couldn't have worked out any better."

Katherine was in shock, feeling totally disillusioned. This had to be nothing more than a very bad dream. It could not actually be happening. She looked at Ruth, bewildered.

"What I don't understand is why would you think my grandpa was going to pass away anytime soon. I mean, you take wonderful care of him and are very loving toward him. You make sure he eats a healthy diet, and you are vigilant about making sure he takes his medications. I even saw the record you're keeping when you take his blood pressure. Those are not the actions of a person who wants someone to die."

Ruth threw her head back, laughing. "Those pills I chase him down with every day ain't nothing but sugar pills. When I pick up his prescriptions, I dump out what's in the bottles and refill them with useless pills. As for his healthy diet, that's not true either. I tell him I cook healthy, but in reality, I make his food just about as unhealthy as I can. I was worried you'd pick up on it when you had that dessert I made last week cause I heard you were an excellent cook, but you didn't."

"I'm still confused, Ruth. If you caused my grandpa's death, almost everything would have gone to me. How were you going to convince me to give it to you?"

"You're the one detail I hadn't quite figured out yet. You lived too far away. After the accident, it all got easier. Do you think that rattler got there all by itself? I saw you leave on your ride and made that plan for when you got back. Released it from the bag at just the right time, too. Then that Russell spoiled it, saving your life. Well, there's nobody here but just the two of us. I can take care of getting rid of you right now, and then my plan will be complete." She raised the poker, intending to use it as a weapon to bash it into Katherine's head.

"Ruth, WAIT! If you kill me, someone will know. It will be obvious."

"I haven't come this far to give up now, my sweet Katherine. After I bash your head in, I'm going to drag your body over to that stone fireplace hearth, making it look like you fell and hit your head against it, causing your death. Say goodnight, Katherine. Sorry, it has to end like this." She moved fast, swinging the poker. Katherine let out a piercing scream and tried to dodge it, but it was too late. Ruth had made contact with Katherine's skull. Blood flowed. Then she raised the poker high over her head to strike Katherine again for good measure to make sure she was dead.

"Drop it, Ruth!" She turned to see Russ standing just inside the door with his gun pointed directly at her. He had heard the scream from where he'd been working by the porch step.

"Well, well, well... the knight in shining armor shows up again. You're too late this time, but it's just my good fortune. This time, I get two for the price of one." She re-angled the poker and took a swing at him at the same moment that he pulled the trigger. The bullet landed directly in the center of her chest, killing her on contact.

He pulled out his cell phone as he was going to Katherine's side. There was a lot of blood surrounding her head.

"911, what's your emergency?"

"This is Russell Woodson. I need an ambulance and the police at the O'Neill estate. There's been a shooting and an attempted murder."

Using his training from the Secret Service, Russ did what he could to keep Katherine alive until the paramedics got there. At least she had a pulse, and he had used pressure on her head wound to try to stop the bleeding. When the paramedics and police got there, it was complete chaos. The paramedics were busily attending to Katherine. They had confirmed that Ruth was dead, and they covered her body with a sheet. The police were talking with Russ just outside the house. Ben had heard the sirens and commotion, causing him to head back to the house. When Russ saw him approaching the house, he held out his arm and stopped him.

"You shouldn't go in there, Ben. It's quite a scene. I'll be able to explain everything to you later."

The paramedics were rushing out the door with Katherine on a stretcher and an IV and oxygen were already in place.

Ben ran to the back of the ambulance, "Would someone

please tell me what's happened here and what's happened to my Katie?!"

Russ tried to calm him down, reassuring him that Katherine was going to be just fine, although he did not know if she would be. She had lost an enormous amount of blood. Just before they closed the doors of the ambulance, Ben ran over, climbing in the back. "You're not going anywhere without me."

After Ruth's body had been removed, the Sergeant told Russ he would need to come down to the station to give him a statement. All he wanted was to go to the hospital, but knowing law enforcement as he did, he obliged. He had, after all, just shot someone and killed them. Even though he had a tight bond with the police force and had told them what happened, he knew the protocol, whether or not it was self-defense. He got in his truck and followed them to the station.

Russ had just finished giving them his statement about what had happened, which felt like it took hours, even though it hadn't. All he could think of was Katherine.

The investigator saw him on his way out and stopped him. "We got back the results from the prints we pulled from Mrs. Sandston's car. One distinct set stood out, not matching any of the others that were pulled from the brakes. They belonged to Ruth O'Reilly. It appears that someone had tampered with the brake fluid, causing the brakes to fail."

Russ got in his truck and made a B-line to the hospital. He had to know if Katherine had survived. There had been so much blood, and her pulse had been weak. He entered the emergency room and gave the attendant at the desk her name. She motioned over to exam room four. When he entered the exam room, the nurse was removing the blood-stained sheet but looked up at him.

"Excuse me," Russ said, "could you tell me where the woman is that was in this room?"

"You're too late. She's gone."

He had been too late. Katherine was dead. He just stood there motionless, feeling empty. It was as if the wind had gone out of his sails and his emotions were drained. He had only felt this way once before, and that was when he'd lost his wife and unborn child. He had tried to fight the attraction he had for Katherine. She had been like a magnet, pulling him toward her. They had a chemistry that he could not deny, but now it was too late. He would never be able to tell her.

He heard a noise behind him and turned. Katherine was sitting in a wheelchair, being pushed back into the room by an orderly.

Russ ran to her, falling on his knees in front of her. Tears had formed in his eyes. He reached up, wrapping his arms around her, tightly holding her.

"Katherine, oh, Katherine, I thought you didn't make it. I thought I'd missed my chance to tell you." Then he pulled back just far enough to look into her inviting, whiskey-colored eyes. Even with her bandaged head, she was, at this moment, the most beautiful woman he'd ever seen.

Katherine looked down at him, smiling warmly. "I came back because I forgot something. Tell me what, Russ?"

"I have fallen in love with you, Katherine. I tried to fight it, but I no longer can. You came into my life for a reason, and I'd like to explore that reason with you."

Katherine placed her hands on his arms, bracing to stand up. She gazed into his eyes. "I love you too, Russ. I never thought I'd say that to a man again, but I do. I'm certain of it."

He couldn't remember ever being happier. He took her in his arms for a long, delicious Kiss.

Ben re-entered the room and saw them kissing. He stood just behind them, smiling broadly, exclaiming, "Well, it's about time."

"Grandpa, what do you mean by that?"

"I've felt for quite some time that the two of you were meant for each other. Why do you think I kept thinking of ways to throw you together?"

She went over and hugged him. "Oh, Grandpa. You've always known me better than I knew myself. I love you so very much."

"I love you too, my sweet Katie. The doctor will be signing your release papers and then let's say we get you out of here."

He walked a little ahead of them when they were leaving. Katherine and Russ were walking out arm-in-arm. She looked at him sideways, saying, "How did you know what Ruth was up to?"

"I didn't know exactly what she was up to, but I knew she was not who she pretended to be. I told you..... I have a set of special skills. I'm trained to be able to read people."

Katherine stopped walking and turned to him. She kissed him, looked into his eyes, and said, "Oh, I think you have a lot of other special skills."

With Katherine's statement to the police at the hospital and Russ's at the station, the charges against Chris were dropped and they released him. After leaving Sophie with Katherine and Ben, his parents picked him up and took him directly to the hospital. They remained in the hallway so he could go in and see Melanie alone. He ran to her bedside and leaned down, wrapping his arms around her, sobbing. "Oh, Mel. I'm so sorry. I'm sorry for so many things. I didn't mean any of those things I said to you. I love you so much. Please forgive me."

"I love you too, Chris. I need to explain what happened to you."

"I don't care what happened, or about those pictures. All I care about is you, Sophie, and our life together."

"Chris?"

"Yes, Baby."

"Right before the accident, my life flashed before my eyes. All I saw was you and Sophie, and that's the only thing I want."

He leaned down and gave her a gentle kiss on the lips and even gentler little kisses to all the bruises on her face.

When Ben, Katherine, and Russ returned home from the hospital, Russ walked over to Katherine after she got out of Ben's car.

With a saddened expression, he said, "I guess you'll be going home soon now that Melanie's going to be alright."

She wrapped her arms around his waist. "I think I am home. This is where I belong. Besides, I think I need to give the man who saved my life twice a chance."

"Actually, that would be three times." She looked at him, confused. "That night when the storm was coming after your husband's funeral, I was checking on the property and found you on the beach. I picked you up and carried you to the guest house where you were staying."

"I remember wanting to die. I felt myself being lifted, but I thought I was going to heaven to be with Jason." She looked at him with extreme tenderness. "I'm so glad now that I didn't."

The kiss that followed next was one of tender harmony, and Katherine felt her fate had been sealed. She loved this man. Her past was now where it belonged, and she was ready to start a new journey.

Epilogue

"Push Katherine, push." Katherine was panting heavily, trying with all her might. She had been in labor for ten hours. It would not be much longer, the doctor had said.

They had been married six months after they met. It had been a quiet ceremony on the beach, with only Melanie, Chris, Sophie, and Ben in attendance. The damage Ruth had done to Ben's already weak heart shortened his life, and he passed away shortly thereafter. Katherine took comfort in knowing that he was with her grandmother now, looking down on them. She was at peace with it.

"One more big push, Katherine," the Doctor said. "You're about to see your baby."

Katherine was crying tears of sheer joy and so was Russ. She pushed as hard as she could and then heard the cries from their baby boy.

"You're almost there, Katherine. Do that for me one more time. You're doing great."

Russ was helping to support Katherine's back as she slightly raised herself, groaning and pushing, and then it was over.

"Congratulations, Mr. & Mrs. Woodson. You have a healthy baby boy and a healthy baby girl."

The nurse wrapped them in swaddle blankets and brought them over to the joyous couple. They were half crying and half laughing. These were the most extreme emotions either of them had ever felt. Russ was looking at Katherine with so much love and pride. She had been so brave.

"Well, my love," he said, "What should we name our two bundles of joy?"

"What do you think about Benjamin and Elizabeth?"

"I can't think of any names that would be more perfect."

* * *

They had been home for a week. They decorated Katherine's childhood room for Elizabeth and Melanie's across the hall for Benjamin. They were enormously happy. The doorbell rang.

Katherine was so tired. The neighbors and others in the community had meant well and had been dropping off food and gifts for days, but she really didn't want to see anybody right now.

"Honey, can you just tell whoever it is that I'm laying down? I'm just too exhausted to see anyone."

"Oh, I think this is one guest you're going to want to see." He went over to open the door.

When Katherine saw who was standing there, her face broadened into a wide smile, and she fled toward them.

She wrapped her arms around him, holding him in a tight hug. "Stewart! I can't believe you're here." Then she let go and looked at the woman standing next to him. She went to her with the warmest of warm smiles, reaching out her arms to her. "Mildred." That's all she needed to say. She and Mildred had formed that once-in-a-lifetime special bond that required no words between them.

"Katherine, my dear, you are absolutely glowing. Motherhood apparently agrees with you."

"I've never been happier, Mildred. Now please, you two, come into the parlor and sit down. You must be exhausted after such a long drive."

Stewart chuckled. "Oh, we didn't drive heah Katherine. I flew us down in my plane and then rented a vehicle. Speaking of that, Russ, do you think you could help me with something?"

Stewart and Russ got up and walked outside.

"Stu's an excellent pilot, Katherine, and it was just lovely seeing everything from the air on the way down."

When they came back in through the door, they were each carrying a tiny wooden cradle. They brought them in and set them on the rug in front of where she and Mildred were sitting.

Katherine looked at them in amazement. She knew he had made them for her. The type of carpentry looked very much like some of the other things he had shown her he'd made. She got down on her knees in front of them. On the curved end of each one, he'd carved each of their names, Benjamin and Elizabeth. She touched the letters of the names with her fingers, just as she had touched the carving he had hung on her patio wall so long ago. She got up and went to him with tears in her eyes, hugging him, unable to say anything.

They stayed for several hours, visiting and holding the babies.

"So, how is Muffin?" Katherine asked Stewart

Chuckling, he answered. "Oh, he's doing just fine. He's my little shadow."

"I'm so happy he's with you, Stewart. He's loved you from the moment he met you."

"The feeling is mutual."

Katherine got a ton of pictures. Watching Stewart holding her daughter gave her an idea.

"Stewart, you've always been much like a father to me. Would it be alright if my children call you Grandpa?"

This time, Stewart's eyes were filled with tears. "I'd be honared, Katherine."

"Why don't the two of you stay here while you're in town? We have a couple of empty rooms and the guest house as well."

"Thank you for the offah Katherine, but a nice little bed-and-breakfast caught our eye on the way heah. We'll stay thaya but we'll see you again befowah we go back."

Katherine and Russ stood on the porch, waving to Stewart and Mildred as they pulled away. Russ was behind her with his arms wrapped around her waist. After they were gone, he looked around at her sideways, noticing the serene smile on her face.

"What's that smile about?"

"I am just so happy, Russ. I don't think I've ever been happier in my life. This is where I am supposed to be, right where my life began. There is just one other thing, though."

"Anything, just name it."

"I've been thinking about starting an herb garden in the yard. I was wondering if you'd build a white picket fence around it?"

"Consider it done, my love."

She turned to face him then, but before she could kiss him, Lizzie let out one of her explosive wails that probably sent wildlife running for cover.

Lowering her face, resting her forehead on his chest, she

said, "I have a feeling that child is always going to speak her mind."

"Hmmm...... I wonder where she gets that from?" Russ said

She gave him a playful, sarcastic look, followed by a quick peck on the lips. Then she took hold of his shirt sleeve, leading him back into the house.

"Come on, Dad. Duty calls."

The End

Acknowledgments

First and foremost, I would like to thank the men and women in our Armed forces for their service. It is because of their great sacrifice; we can sleep soundly in our beds at night. I would also like to thank Officer Dale Kerns of Camp Lejeune for his wealth of information and support given to the Marines and their families.

I must admit I have a special place in my heart for the Marines because my son served in the Marines, and I am so extremely proud of him for that accomplishment. I learned from that experience with him why they say The few, The Proud, The Marines. I learned that you don't just sign up to join the Marines; you must become one. To earn the eagle globe and anchor being placed in the palm of your hand, you must endure training that reshapes your heart, body, and soul.

When I set out on this journey, I had a plan for my book. It was supposed to be an entirely fictional book other than references to real people, events, establishments, organizations, or locales intended only to provide a sense of authenticity.

Little by little, however, in certain instances, I found myself drawing from the early days of my childhood and/or other life experiences for inspiration. Many of them were just a natural fit. Like Katherine, I grew up with a cousin a few months apart in age, and we were very close. While she was not Melanie's character, like Melanie, she was much more comfortable with nature's creatures than I was. She would have reached into that bucket to grab her own minnow when fishing with Ben. I have a photo of the two of us at around the age of five standing a few apart, with me having a look of horror on my face as she was reaching out to me, tantalizing me, holding a frog in her hand, and laughing hysterically. Also, like Melanie, as a young girl of about four, I would sneak down in the morning before my Dad left for work. He would make me a cup of coffee (warm milk) to sit at the table and have with him. I was his little buddy and absolutely adored him.

Now, my grandmother was nothing like Elizabeth, as my grandmother was raised in North Carolina and was very much a country girl; however, they had much in common. My Grandmother was a fabulous seamstress. I remember the brides coming to her home for their fittings and thinking they looked like Cinderella. She also made quilts out of our outgrown dresses. She had a beautiful rose garden, letting me watch as she pruned them. One of my fondest memories is her cooking. She would give me a basket, take my tiny little hand, and walk to the grapevines. She let me help pick them, and then we'd go back to the house and make jelly. I was quite young, so she folded and tied an apron around my waist. I would watch her cook the grapes in a large pot, and then she'd put them in a large sack and let me help her squish them. Her cooking was incredible, and everything she made was delightful. I'm fairly certain, though, that it would have given a Cardiologist a coronary because I'm sure lard, butter, whole milk, and salt were constant staples she used in her dishes.

I am so grateful for my memories, some of which did not resurface until I was writing this book. I believe our memories and experiences in life make us who we are and help to keep family bonds strong.